RIDING BY NIGHT,
SLEEPING BY DAY,
SLOCUM THOUGHT HE WAS FINALLY SAFE.
THEN HE MET UP WITH LETTY PRAY.

Slocum awoke the afternoon of the third day, his spirit buoyed by having evaded capture so far. He ran a hand over his week-old beard, grateful that it changed his appearance, and headed west, riding some 200 yards parallel to the main road. Rounding a sandstone outcropping lacerated by wind and weather and crowned with three stunted oaks, he came upon a man straddling the right foreleg of a handsome big-beamed bay. He stood, examining its hoof, letting it drop at Slocum's approach and looking up.

It was no man but a lovely woman, an eye-stopping beauty with a complexion like cream, sparkling green eyes and golden hair tucked up under her Tower Stetson.

"He seems to have picked up a stone."

Slocum pulled up and dismounted. "Let's have a look."

It was a pebble the size of the tip of his little finger. It had lodged between the buttress and the shoe. Using the tongue of his belt buckle, he pried it loose easily.

"It may be sore for a day or so, but it's nothing serious," he said, letting the hoof drop. "You can ride him okay." She stood watching him. Straightening up, he turned to her, smiling.

His face froze. In her hand was a chrome-plated .38 pointed straight at his heart.

JAKE LOGAN

SEE TEXAS AND DIE

SEE TEXAS AND DIE

Cover illustration by Bart Jerner.

Published simultaneously in the United States and Canada by Playboy Press, Chicago, Illinois. Printed in the United States of America. Library of Congress Catalog Card Number: 77-93129. First edition.

Books are available at quantity discounts for promotional and industrial use. For further information, write our sales-promotion agency: Ventura Associates, 40 East 49th Street, New York, New York 10017.

ISBN 0-872-16458-6

1

Slocum lay back down on the bed, spreading his legs, letting her thrust herself between them. Lowering her blond head, she gulped in his cock and began massaging the underside of it with her warm wet tongue, quickly getting it as stiff as a round-top rail spike.

"You got yourself some mouthful, cowboy," she said, releasing his head, raising her eyes, winking and grinning.

"Can we save the chatter 'til after?" asked Slocum between clenched teeth holding back his ball-burst. Laughing gaily, she went back down on him, driving her mouth to the base, holding it there and thrashing it wildly with her tongue. To Slocum it felt like fire suddenly flaming up, a blaze to boil his balls and shoot 'em loose clear up into her brain. Now she began moving her naked body, her magnificent tits swinging, whack-slapping each other as she shifted over his upraised right knee to his side, then back over the other way, all the while locking his cock with the ring of her lips, punishing it mercilessly with her flailing tongue.

Then she started up with agonizingly beautiful slowness, drawing the boiling come from his balls, up the conduit to the head. Pulsing forth, it splattered against the roof of her mouth, flooding her cheeks, cascading down her throat. The room whirled, the bed seemed to float upward and the iron footrail beyond her ass melted in a haze as his eyes glazed over and he sighed loudly.

When she finally released his cock, letting it slump down onto his spent balls, there wasn't a trace of come to be seen. Every drop, he concluded, was well on its way to digestion.

"Stop panting, cowboy. That was just the old Saturday night one-dollar special. Nothing to write home about."

"I got four more bucks where that one's coming from, lady."

"June. June Honeywell." She indicated her mouth. "Get it?"

"Four more," he repeated, unable to conceal his eagerness.

"You reckon you can get up four more loads worth the whipping out?"

"Gimme thirty seconds. Just you rest your whip."

Again she laughed, bouncing up out of bed, creaking the springs loudly, her massive breasts again slapping away, attacking each other.

"It's your money. I'm thirsty; let's have a drink."

"I got no money for rotgut," said Slocum flatly, drawing his feet together, setting them on the bare floor and sitting up. "My stomach's been ailing lately and I got to baby it."

"Horseshit! This ain't gonna cost you nothing. It's part o' the service."

"It ain't the cost. It's the wear and tear."

"Mister, you taste one glass you'll want the whole bottle. You'll see."

She stood at the commode, pouring into two fat tumblers from an unlabeled gallon jug that looked to Slocum as if it had been dragged through a hog wallow. Rising to his feet, he studied the white-enamel top of the commode. It was spotted with at least a dozen discolorations in various sizes that looked like burns.

"What you got burned the top o' that thing?" he asked. "Acid?"

"Ha!" In the process of raising her tumbler to her lips, she paused halfway and poured a few drops onto the surface. But instead of bubbling up as he half expected, it sat there as harmless as spilt water.

"You're a fuckin' caution, you know that, June?"

She handed him his glass and he sipped it slowly. It was like a branding iron rammed down his gullet, bouncing against the floor of his gut, flaring outward in all directions and climbing the walls.

"Sweet Jesus, what in hell is this, snake venom?"

"Whiskey. Me and sister Elsie and sister Hazel make it ourselves. Our pappy died and left us his still. Wasn't that grand o' him?"

"You might run a little kerosene through the worm to clean the rust outta the damned thing." He studied the glass. "Moon. How about that?"

"I do believe that's what they call it in Georgia."

"Must be two hundred proof."

"Can't say. We just cook it and drink it to perk ourselves up." So saying, she emptied her glass down her throat, raised the tumbler in triumph and beamed broadly. "Drink up, it's just what the doctor ordered for ailing guts."

He drank slowly, letting his innards become used to the pitiless onslaught of the stuff. He hoped it was getting by his teeth without melting them and that his stomach lining wasn't being chewed away like a beef bone in a starving mongrel's jaws. He finished a second helping, having decided that for something so strong it didn't go down half bad once a body got used to it. He was sitting on the edge of the bed, watching her pour, when she suddenly wiped away the few drops spilled earlier on the enamel top.

And there it was: a scar like the others.

"Jesus!" exclaimed Slocum over her laughter, dropping his empty glass to the floor and heeling it. "You're the craziest bitch I ever did meet!"

"You think I'm crazy you ought to see my two sisters. Hey, what about them two buddies o' yours?"

"What about what?"

"You work with 'em?"

"Yup."
"Doing what, robbin' banks and stagecoaches?"
"Like hell. We been up to Kansas City the past six months freighting, busting our humps filling and emptying box cars."
"That's no work for a man, that's for a jackass."
"You're lookin' at one."
"Any money in freighting?"
"Helluva lot more than booting hides."
"Down to the bar, that whiskey-nosed little redheaded fella mentioned you and him was in the war together."
"Yeah. That's old Jay Packer. One o' the best o' the good ol' boys. Damned decent soldier. Don't let him being short fool you none. He can pull down a fifteen-hundred-pound steer in two shakes and bust a guy twice his size into little-sized pieces before you can pick up your hat. I've seen him."
"He's a funny sort. You two with the Union or the losers?"
Slocum's eyes narrowed. "Watch your mouth, June Bug. I got what you might call sentimental attachments to the Confederacy. Just like old Jay has."
"Who's the other fella?"
"Race Turnbull. We met him on the job. Real name's Horace, but he calls himself Race."
"Can't say I blame him. What's your name?"
"Smith, Louis."
"Well, Louis, you got some fine bellrope 'twixt them skinny pins o' yours."
"It's been askin' after you."
"Has it now?"
Crossing back to the bed she went down on her knees and taking his balls in hand began massaging them gently. "Got to load the cannon afore you can shoot it, right?"
"Yeah."
Suddenly he didn't feel so good. Not sick—more dizzy, light-headed, as if his brains had dropped out of his skull and down his throat into his chest.

"What's the trouble, Louis? You're all of a sudden looking pale as a fish!"

"I—"

The room spun, everything within view liquefying, swimming. Then down he fell, out cold before his back even hit the bed.

2

The early afternoon sun came pouring in over the batwing doors, shining up the footrail at the bar full length and bouncing brightly off the spittoon. Six or seven locals stood at the bar in various stages of sobriety, no one speaking, all of them seemingly lost in thought. All wore dust-caked chaps or denims, except the drinker nearest the doors. In spite of the heat, he was splendidly attired in an obviously expensive Prince Albert, a well-brushed black *sombrero*, gray pants without a wrinkle neatly tucked into burnished black boots and a white silk shirt that shone like a pearl when the sun hit it. He was not wearing a gun.

As he stood nursing a glass of rye, a wretched-looking stray dog ventured in, lifted one leg ceremoniously and deposited his signature against the jamb. Seeing this, the bartender became so angry he flung the glass he was polishing at the beast, chasing it back out into the street.

It was a hot, lazy, spiritless day, the sort of hourstring that any man with common sense dozes through in preference to exerting effort, even the minuscule amount necessary to sustain conversation.

The three men playing matchstick poker at a disreputable-looking table in the back of the Prayerville Palace, however, appeared to lack the common sense the weather demanded. Their angers were up and audible.

"It was your goddamned fault, Packer," said Turnbull sullenly. "You was the one wanted to pick them three bitches up."

Jap Packer snorted, shifted his feet and tossed another match into the pot. "Call. I notice you didn't back away from the idee. You was as ready to get serviced as me and John. Christ, your tongue was hanging out a foot."

"How in hell was I supposed to know they'd up and feed us free booze spiked with pizen?"

"How was I?"

"It wasn't poisoned," said Slocum mildly, showing a brace of aces against Turnbull's jacks and hauling the pot to his pile. "It was some kind o' knockout powder. Mine slipped it to me between drinks, I reckon. What kills me is I was so all-fired worried about how powerful the damned stuff was, I never did dream she was out to knock me cold."

"It sure enough beats all," said Packer. "I been robbed afore, but I was always awake when it happened. Two hundred and forty bucks, every damned cent I got in the world. Except the two bucks she laid on my forehead."

"How long do you figure you was out?" asked Slocum of Turnbull.

"Couple hours, maybe three, through sundown and into dark. Just enough time for 'em to clear outta town. I still say that goddamned barkeep set us up. Him trying to tell me he never even seen 'em pick us up."

"*We* picked *them* up," said Packer. "Remember?"

"What the hell's the difference?" snapped Turnbull. "Picked up, fucked, sucked, knocked out and robbed, and when we run down and collar him he claims he never even noticed them three. I shoulda broke his lying head into two pieces clean!"

"That sure woulda got us our money back," observed Packer dryly.

"What gets me is we wasted the whole goddamn

day looking for them three, and it's like they disappeared clean off the face o' the earth."

"Wade City," mused Packer aloud. "I'm remembering that name. I'm going back there someday, find them and get that money back. Shit, they must pull that dodge three, four times a week. They likely got more goddamned bucks stashed away than the Leadville Tabors."

"Your deal, Race," said Slocum.

A dreamy look crept into Packer's sparkling green eyes. "What a pair that Hazel did have, though. Man, you coulda fit a size-nine poke bonnet on each one. And what a trap—I thought it was gone for good when I dropped it in."

Turnbull shuffled spiritlessly, Slocum cut, Turnbull dealt and came up with three sixes showing. Packer bucked him with the makings of a big straight, then dropped out and cursed loudly when Turnbull declined to show his full house. Collecting his pot, he scribbled laboriously with his pencil stub on the empty grocery bag at his right forearm.

"Two thousand two hundred," he said as he wrote. "Carry the two, add the four makes forty-two thousand even you owe me."

"What the hell you talking about, forty-two thousand!" exclaimed Packer irritably. "Christ Almighty, it was only thirty-eight five before you dealt the goddamned hand! Lemme see that!" Snatching up the bag, he ran down the figures, his lips moving noticeably. "Just like I thought, you don't even know how to add, you goddamned crook!"

"Who you calling a crook?" burst Turnbull, rising from his chair.

"Relax, you two, dammit all!" snapped Slocum. "We're only playing for matches."

"That ain't the point!" exclaimed Packer. "It's the damned principle of the thing. I don't cotton to card cheats!"

"Then you keep the fuckin' score!" Turnbull waved away the bag and pencil.

"Like hell," said Slocum. "He can't add worth a shit, neither. To hell with the score, let's just play."

"You know something, Packer?" said Turnbull. "Some day you're gonna open that big mouth o' yours oncet too often and I'm gonna tie your goddamned whiskers to your head hair and shut you up for permanent!"

"You try it, and I'll kick your asshole forty feet off your shanks!"

"Shut up, the two o' you," said Slocum, annoyed.

They played in heavy silence for a few minutes, the cards slapping the table, the matches moving about. Slocum took two hands running with queens and a little straight and broke the silence with a question.

"How much money they leave us?"

"Two bucks apiece," said Packer. "Six bucks."

"Less than that counting these here drinks," remarked Turnbull. "It's close on three hundred fifty miles to Eagle Pass, three hundred fifty miles on five bucks and change."

"We got to decide here and now," said Slocum. "I say we draw lots and the loser sells his rifle."

"Bullshit, little Eva!" snapped Packer. "You sell yours if you like, but I got me a new Colt Stagecoach Rim-Fire. Cost me a damned pretty penny, and I ain't about to let it go for biscuits and coffee!"

"What do you say to selling all three saddles?" asked Turnbull. "We could easy enough bareback it to Eagle Pass. It ain't like we had to climb the Rockies. And selling all three saddles plays fair with everybody."

"Not bad thinking," said Packer. "What do you say, John?"

"I say forget it. I happen to have the best saddle I ever owned, and I got no inclination to part with it."

"You're talking like it was a woman," began Turnbull. "A saddle's only a saddle."

"Like hell, mister. This here one's genuine oiled California skirting leather, sixteen-inch tree, steel fork—"

"Steel?" asked Packer.

Slocum nodded. "Hide covered, wool-lined skirts, steel strainer, beaded roll cantle—"

"All right, all right," said Turnbull. "But we got to peddle something, dammit!"

A shadow fell across the table and all three looked up. It was the well-dressed stranger, touching the brim of his *sombrero* in greeting, smiling in a friendly way.

"Beg your pardon, gentlemen, any chance of a stranger joining the play?"

"If you got matches," said Packer quietly. "We're new in town. We sorta hesitate to flash around our wads."

"Yeah," said Slocum, "all five dollars and change."

"The name is Porter Fairchild," the stranger said, pulling up a chair and sitting. Introductions followed. "I confess I couldn't help overhearing part of your conversation, and it occurred to me you might be interested," he said, lowering his head and his voice—"in a business proposition."

"What business?" asked Slocum, his dark eyes fastened on Fairchild, who glanced about. The bartender was busy straightening his bottles against the mirror. The patrons at the bar continued their drinking in silence, ignoring one another. The stray dog was standing outside, wagging his chopped-off tail, evidently readying for a second assault on the door jamb.

"I suggest we find someplace with a bit more privacy," said Fairchild. Getting up, he approached the bartender, spoke briefly with him, returned to the table and escorted Slocum and the others into a room in the rear, closing and bolting the door behind them.

"Where you boys heading?" he asked. "Did I hear you say Eagle Pass?"

"There's jobs down there," said Packer.

"But to get down there you need eating money, is that it?" They nodded and exchanged glances. It was apparent that none of the three was completely sold on the newcomer, and the particular look in Slocum's eyes announced that Fairchild had best get to the point before he lost their attention altogether. Reading John's eyes, Fairchild reacted positively.

"Gentlemen, I am prepared to pay you two hundred dollars for about ten minutes' work."

"Two hundred!" Packer's eyes grew wide as saucers, and his beard dropped.

"Apiece."

Turnbull laughed. "What in hell you want us to do, mister, rob a bank?"

"Not *a* bank, *my* bank."

Turnbull stopped laughing.

"I happen to be president of the Farmers and Merchants Bank in Goodnight, a little town about three miles west of here. Perhaps I should explain."

"That might help," said Slocum evenly. Mr. Porter Fairchild was not drunk so he must be playing games. Still, hearing him out couldn't hurt any.

"Reposing in my safe is an envelope containing a parcel of railroad stocks. The Southern Pacific–Texas and Pacific line. I would very much like to get my hands on that envelope."

"How come you don't just reach in and grab?" asked Turnbull.

Fairchild shook his head, smiling tolerantly. "There's a better way, Horace. If the bank is broken into, the safe blown, the place wrecked and the stocks are missing, nobody can possibly blame yours truly. So you see, I need your help. All that's required is to 'open' the safe, get that envelope and deliver it to me at a predetermined spot. I'll hand you two hundred dollars apiece, cash money."

Slocum stifled a yawn, leaned back in his chair and fish-eyed Fairchild. Packer's eyes went to the tabletop, the pink flesh of his brow wrinkling tightly in confusion. Turnbull appeared most impressed with the offer.

"I think you got the wrong three fellas here, Mr. Fairchild," said Slocum evenly. "We may look green to you, but you can take my word we been around the barn. Shit, mister, we don't even know you're what you claim to be, do we now? I mean president of the bank."

"That shouldn't be too difficult to check, John," said Fairchild.

"He's got you there," said Packer.

Slocum was not amused. "That's the least of it," he continued. "I mean you said your piece less than a minute ago, and already I can see seven hundred holes in the deal. Number one, if we did go in—and I ain't saying for two seconds *I* would—what if we're caught? You sure as hell wouldn't alibi us, you'd be a damned fool to."

"That's so," said Turnbull. "You could be wanting to set us up for a damned double cross."

Fairchild shook his head. "I could be, but I'm not."

"So you say," said Slocum. "Another thing, how can you be sure we wouldn't steal that envelope and ride off in the opposite direction?"

"That you'd never do. Those stocks would be worthless to you. You see, I happen to be the legal transfer agent. My name is on every certificate under the rightful owner's name. So only he or I can convert them. All I'd need do is forge his name."

"Yeah, well, all that's mighty interesting," said Slocum, "and I can't speak for these two, but you can count me out, firm and final. I ain't about to contract to rob no bank. Not that I got sentiments against busting the law. But if I was to hold up any bank I'd pick the place and the time all by myself. I sure enough wouldn't hire out for it."

"Two hundred dollars for ten minutes' work," repeated Fairchild.

"That's a pile o' bucks, John," said Packer.

"There's no risk," added the banker, "nobody'll be around. You can kick in the back door or go in through a window. Blow the safe, grab the envelope and get out. I say ten minutes though it'll probably be closer to two or three."

"It sounds mighty appealing to me, John," said Turnbull.

Slocum produced a cheroot from his shirt pocket, lit it, puffed and shook his head slowly. "Like I said, too many holes. If you two are that smitten with it, go and get at it. You don't need this ol' boy."

"No thanks," said Packer. "Either we're all in or we're all out."

Turnbull nodded, then turned to Fairchild. "How about you giving us a couple days to talk it over? Could you?"

"By all means."

"I don't need two days, I don't need two minutes. You guys can count in if you like, but not me." Slocum turned to counting his matches.

Fairchild got up, his chair scraping the floor loudly, signaling that the meeting was at an end. "Two days. Only one thing, if you do decide to take the job, I'd appreciate it if you didn't show your faces in Goodnight, that is, not before the time set to do the job." Taking out an expensive-looking watch, he held it up. "Two-thirty Thursday, forty-eight hours from now. We can meet again right here in this room, fair enough?"

"Fair enough," said Turnbull.

Fairchild left. The moment he was out the door Packer and Turnbull began hurling arguments in favor of acceptance at Slocum. He sat listening politely, drawing slowly on his smoke, tapping the ashes to the floor.

"You know what your trouble is, you two?" he asked finally. "You both got a tendency to get your mouths working without hooking 'em up to your brains.

I mean forget suspicions, just listening to what the man said is enough to turn me off. It's plain as day: the reason he don't want us to show up there is because we'd find out he's no more president of that bank than I am. He's nothing more than a smooth-talking holdup sort himself, out to palm the risk off this time around."

"He sure ain't dressed, he sure don't talk or act like no holdup man," observed Turnbull. "And I still say checking whether he is or ain't the president has got to be easy as rolling off a fat whore." He winked. "There's something else I'm thinking about, too. If we was to open that safe, there'd have to be bucks in there, wouldn't there? We could load ourselves up, give him his dumb envelope, collect the six hundred and ride ass to Wyoming faster than three scared jackrabbits."

"That's bone stupid, Race," responded Slocum, sucking his cheroot. "You're doing it again, talking without thinking. I still say you two are missing the big fly in the damned salve. It's plain as day he's fixing to set us poor assholes up to take the pressure off himself."

"What pressure is that?" asked Packer.

"Who in hell knows? Who cares?" Slocum's patience was beginning to wear thin. More and more obvious was the fact that he was unable to propose nearly as many reasons against accepting Fairchild's offer as Packer and Turnbull were producing in favor of it. "Let's not kid ourselves, if it ever comes down to a shout-out, his word against ours, we'd be dead!"

"All right, all right," snapped Turnbull in a disgusted tone. "So we don't take the job. What do we do for traveling bucks?"

"Hold your goddamn horses!" exclaimed Packer. "Who says we don't take the job?"

"Almighty God, John Slocum, who else?" Turnbull snorted, turning away from Slocum almost as if sight of him was suddenly making him sick to his stomach.

Packer hauled out argument after argument in favor of acceptance. The brevity of the risk time, the assumable fact that a little bend in the road like Goodnight would likely have a cracker box for a safe in its one and only bank, the suggestion that one of them stand guard outside with the mounts ready to sprint, and a good deal more.

"So what do you say, John?" asked Turnbull at length. "You with us or against us?"

"I ain't against *you*, I'm against *it*, dammit! I'd like to sleep on it one night." Stumping his cheroot out on the table, he let it lay a moment, then snapped it against the far wall with his index finger.

"We got us two whole days," said Packer. "We'll all sleep on it."

Slocum turned to him. "What'd you think o' that fella, Jay?"

Packer shrugged. "He looked to be harmless. Friendly sort."

"Too goddamned friendly, if you ask me."

Turnbull scoffed at this. "Mister, you're looking for ghosts under the bed. He's no damned different than any other bank type I ever met. I got a sister out Seminole way married to the same sort—fine duds, shiny buckle, big words, clean fingernails, but knows the banking business backwards and forwards."

"That don't impress me none," said Slocum. "All the bankers I ever knew was crooks. Just as crooked as Mr. Porter Fairchild confesses to being. Jesus Christ, can you imagine a man coming up to you, tipping his hat and politely asking you to rob his own bank?"

"There's only one thing sits wrong with me," said Packer thoughtfully.

"What?" asked Slocum.

"The man wants to hire us, talks two hundred bucks apiece, you'd think the least he'd do would be to stand us a bottle."

There was a knock at the door. Turnbull opened it. It was the bartender holding a full quart of Valley Tan.

"Compliments of the gentleman who just left, boys. You want I should bring in your glasses?"

3

Slocum slept that night with a one-dollar redhead named Francey. She devoured him like an experienced pro, hurting him just enough to overload his balls, but not enough to make him yell out loud. Still, she turned out to be the laziest screw he'd ever poked cock into. Not so much as a jiggle, jaggle, joggle or jerk of her ass or any other bare part. She lay under him chewing raisins and snuffling a cold back up into her head, grinning like a road-show clown and grunting every time he tickled her fancy. Had it not been for these four efforts, however, he would have had to assume that she'd either fallen asleep on him or died.

Her room was aglow in pale crimson—chintz curtains, flowered wallpaper and all—thanks to a sheet of red isinglass wound around the lamp and fixed in place with a hair ribbon.

There was little conversation between them, Slocum preferring to anchor his thoughts on Fairchild's offer until he came. No sooner was he pumped clean when Francey began bouncing her ass up and down like a wild mustang first time under leather.

"What the hell ails you!" he snapped. "I already blowed. I got nothing to give you but soft!"

"Oh, my mistake."

He got up, hauled on his drawers, tossed a dollar on the bed and stomped out, muttering, into the hall—only to discover that against the wall was the dustiest, dirtiest, tiredest-looking lot of manhood he'd seen in years. Some held dollar bills, others bottles and one a box of what looked to be peppermint candy.

"Jesus Christ, fella," said an old-timer fronting the herd, "you sure took your own sweet time!"

"What in hell is this?"

"It's Francey night, what do you think it is?"

Slocum gawked at him in bewilderment. The man indicated the long line behind him. "This here be the Triple-K crew outta El Paso. We allus stop over to see Francey, ain't that so, fellas?" The line nodded as one man.

"Christ Almighty, if this don't beat all!" burst Slocum angrily. "First man in on a goddamned gangbang!"

They laughed and grinned down the line that stretched to the lobby of the Hotel Prayerville. At least 40 hands, by Slocum's rough estimate. Oh well, he reflected, at least she hadn't knocked him out and stolen his cash. As if he had any.

Turnbull and Packer were standing at the Palace Bar, nursing ten-cent whiskey, when he walked in. The place was crammed with people: drovers, locals, gents, bums and painted ladies with tits to equal those weighing down June Honeywell and her sneaky sisters.

"Did you take a buck outta the wad?" asked Packer pointedly. "And if so, what for?"

"To get my damned ashes hauled, whatta ya think for?"

"Which brings us down close to four dollars," said Turnbull dejectedly, swiping his blond handlebar moustache with the back of his hand and boring his eyes into his drink.

"It was my goddamn buck!" exclaimed Slocum. "You two act like I stole it!"

Packer smiled. "Was she any good? Was she worth it?"

"Go on over, get in line and see for yourself."

"What the hell does that mean? You mean she's taking on the town?"

"She's taking on the goddamn county!"

"No kidding!"

"Shut the hell up and give me a dime. I need a drink."

Turnbull handed him ten cents, and he got a glass of whiskey. He stood scowling at his image in the glass, sipping the golden brown liquid and seething between swallows.

"What's ailing you, John?" asked Turnbull. "Did you fall in love with her before you found out she bangs gangs?"

"Lay off."

Packer closed in on Slocum, bringing his hairy red face up and searching his eyes. "You decide yet?"

"Yeah, fuck it, let's do it. Only because I'm sick to death o' living broke, sunk down to dollar whores and stuck in this pisshole town."

Turnbull grinned. "That settles it. Day after tomorrow we'll tell him we'll do it."

"Not so fast," said Slocum, "we still got to get a few things straight. Like will he provide us the dynamite to blow the safe, where we're supposed to rendezvous, what we do if the whole scheme blows up in our faces, are we going to get a chance to case the place, fix a clear way out, all the little details."

"We'll get them straight, John," said Packer, "don't you worry none."

"I'll worry right up 'til I get that two hundred bucks in hand and I'm riding out."

"*We're* riding out," said Turnbull. "We're all in it together, the three musketeers."

"Forty guys if there was one!" muttered Slocum coldly.

"What'd you say?" asked both in unison.

"Nothing, not a goddamned thing. Drink up, we got to go check the horses."

4

Inquiring at the Prayerville bank, Slocum established the authenticity of Fairchild's claim to being president of the Goodnight bank. Claiming to be an old acquaintance, he induced a good-natured young kid teller to describe their soon-to-be partner in crime, and the verbal picture that emerged neatly duplicated the one in John's mind.

Fairchild was on time for their meeting in the back room, arriving with a full quart of Taos Lightning, caught and corked in a clean bottle. Their favorable response to his request for help inspired a warm smile and three vigorous handshakes.

"You won't be sorry, fellas."

"You're damned right we won't, mister," said Slocum tightly.

"Do I detect a note of fear?" asked Fairchild. Slocum stared at him. "Concern?"

"That's close to the word."

"John, I'm sure you've heard the expression smooth as silk. Well, let me assure you tomorrow night will be smooth as that. You boys'll find two sticks of Castor dynamite and matches in the trash can behind the bank. When you get the envelope and come out, you're to ride due north about a mile. You'll come to a rise with a dead, stunted oak sitting atop it. Against the moon it looks like an old witch throwing a fit. I'll be there waiting."

"Alone," said Packer.

"Absolutely. I'll pay you then and there, and you'll ride on out. For Eagle Pass, Mexico, Montana, wherever you please. Just get out of the area and stay out."

"That suits us nobly," said Turnbull.

"One last thing," said Slocum.

"What's that, John?" Slocum could never recall seeing anybody quite so relieved as Fairchild looked at that very moment. It was as if somebody had pulled a full-grown bull down off each of his shoulders.

"How about advancing us ten bucks apiece?" asked Slocum. "You know, drinking and stabling money."

Fairchild hesitated, but only briefly, then he went to his wallet, fished out three crisp crackling new ten-dollar bills and handed them each one.

"Thanks," said Slocum.

"A little token of my faith and trust in you boys," Fairchild said. He looked at each in turn. "Anything else?" He paused, waiting. Then he slipped the cork from the bottle, filled four glasses and raised his own in a toast. "To success. Always sweetest when you know it's certain."

"Amen," said Slocum. And everybody drank.

5

The next night the moon and stars shrouded a sky as black as a miner's pocket. It began to rain. First, it came down thrashing in buckets, then letting up, barely splattering the landscape, then the deluge resuming.

The wet weather was welcome to Slocum and the others. Visibility couldn't have been poorer, and the men's only concern was that it might be difficult to find the dead, stunted oak atop the rise where Fairchild would be waiting for his precious envelope.

They reined up behind the bank. Packer dug into the trash can and came up with the dynamite and matches, thoughtfully wrapped in oilskin to keep them dry. He promptly unwrapped them.

"Old Porter is all right people," he observed. "Man's gotta head on his neck."

"You keep holding them fuses high in this wet and we'll need a damned Tillson flare to light 'em," said Slocum sourly. Despite his willingness to join the majority, he was still on edge, his eyes flashing about looking for trouble to jump from every corner.

Packer shoved the dynamite and matches inside his jacket. Then, fisting one gloved hand, he smashed the window and reached in to release the lock.

"Here we go."

"Hold on," said Slocum, "it ain't gonna take three of us to blow a safe. One oughta stick out here with the horses and keep a lookout. You, Jay."

"Suits me, but shake it up. This old poncho of mine's got six holes in it."

The safe proved to be no cracker box, but welded steel with a combination lock and the proud proclamation stamped on the door that it was fireproof.

"Let's just see if the fucking thing is dynamite proof," whispered Turnbull, getting down on his haunches in front of it and readying the dynamite.

"What are you whispering for?" Slocum asked. "Ain't nobody here but us chickens."

"Strike a match."

Slocum did and glanced about. The safe stood flush against a window with file cabinets on either side. Three teller cages in a line stood at their backs, and in the far corner was a small office with "Porter Fairchild—President" neatly lettered in the lower right corner of the glass.

Turnbull nodded and Slocum ignited the fuse.

"Get back," he said.

They scrambled into a corner, covered their ears, held their breaths and watched the fuses sizzle down. Moments later came a thunderous explosion, and a pall of gray-black smoke filled the interior. Rushing through it to the safe they discovered the door hanging at an angle by the top hinge.

"Beautiful!" exclaimed Turnbull. Shoving his hands inside he groped about, coughed away the rapidly thinning smoke and withdrew a large string-bound red manila envelope.

"Let's git," said Slocum.

"One second, let's have us a look."

Turnbull pulled the string and brought out one of the certificates.

"Will you looky here, this one alone is worth five hundred! And hey, there's got to be forty or fifty in here."

"Who gives a shit. They ain't no good to us. Let's get outta here before the whole town shows up!"

He was on his feet and heading toward the window when a 12-pound sledgehammer descended on his hat, flooding his brain with pain and blackness, crumpling him to the floor like a suit slipping off its hanger.

John Slocum hadn't the remotest idea how long he'd been out, but when he came to and could see and hear, his head felt three times normal size and was throbbing so that for an instant he imagined the sledgehammer that felled him was inside his skull short-stroking his brain into a bloody pulp.

Jay Packer lay alongside him, his eyes dazed, his right hand gingerly rubbing the back of his head. Turnbull was nowhere in sight. Others were present, however, standing in a semicircle in front of them, grinning down at them like fun-loving lunatics. All six wore tin stars and the tallest and meanest-looking among them suddenly threw back his head and laughed out loud, his Adam's apple jumping up and down like it was being string-jerked. He knelt down looking from Slocum to Packer to Slocum again.

"Evenin', fellas, welcome to Goodnight."

6

Slocum and Packer shared the same dismal, cramped little cell. They sat on the edges of their wall cots, elbows on their knees, chins planted on the heels of their hands, knuckles pressed against their cheeks. To anyone walking by the cell and looking in, the first impression would have been that neither prisoner was even aware of the other's presence. There had been no noise between them, no verbal abuse of any sort. It wasn't that they weren't on speaking terms, but that each one was ostensibly lost in his own thoughts. Then Slocum broke the spell.

"Turnbull," he said in a tired voice heavy with dejection and tinged with pain from the pigeon-egg–sized bump on the top of his head. "Our buddy. The three musketeers, he called us. We trusted the son of a bitch. So he whomps us on our noggins, runs off, meets Fairchild, delivers the envelope, collects the six hundred and so long, goodbye."

"You really think Fairchild paid him *six* hundred?"

"What I really think is those two was in cahoots all along, with not just the banker man setting us up, but both of 'em. You know something, Jay?"

"Not much, why?"

"Seriously. You know how most everybody got weak flaws in their persons? I mean some are too easily tempted, some can't hold their whiskey, guys can't keep their hands off other guys' wives. You know what my weak flaw is?"

"I can think of a round dozen or so."

"I'm serious, goddammit! My biggest weak flaw is people. I can't read people worth a shit. Every goddamned time the good guy turns out bad and vice-versa. You take that whore June Bug back in Wade City. I coulda bet my life and saddle she was straighter than a taut rope."

"You figured Fairchild right."

"That didn't take no figuring. He proposed a damned crooked deal to us straight out in the first place. I mean he didn't walk up with wings on his back."

"You really think him and Turnbull doubled up to fuck us?"

"Sure as your ass got hair."

Outside the cell, Fairchild stood alongside the sheriff, his eyes hurling fire, his breath coming in short bursts, his nostrils flaring like an overworked bellows.

"On your feet!" he snapped. Packer and Slocum got up facing him. "Now, let's have it, the whole story!"

"You know as much as we do, mister," Slocum said, "maybe lots more. We did exactly like you told us to do, only old Race up and changed the rules at the last minute."

Packer leaned to one side and indicated the top of his head to both men. "That double-dealing bastard was like to bust my skull! I hope you had sense enough not to pay him no six hundred."

"What in hell are you talking about!" yelled Fairchild. "What are you, a moron?"

"Easy, Porter," said the sheriff.

"Easy, my ass. These two jackasses' saddle-tramp friend runs off with twenty thousand dollars' worth of stock certificates, and you're telling me to take it easy?"

"Sheriff," began Slocum, "could we have a word with you alone?"

"Just shut your mouth, Slocum," said Fairchild. "I'll do the talking. All right, where's he heading? Talk, damn you! You tell me, Ty here picks him up with the contents of that envelope intact and you two will be off the hook. Understand?"

"You understand this, you loud-mouthed son of a bitch!" exclaimed Slocum. "You're nothing but a fucking crook no better than the three of us. Worse, it was your idea! Sheriff, this bastard put us up to the whole deal, ain't that so, Jay?"

"That's the gospel truth," said Packer. "We were to steal that envelope outta his safe, hand it over to him and he was supposed to give us two hundred bucks apiece. Only Turnbull double-crossed us."

Slocum pointed at Fairchild, waggling his finger. "He's the one should be in here. He's the damned brains behind this thing. It was all his idea."

"Is there anything in what he says?" the sheriff asked Fairchild, turning to him with a mischievous leer spreading across his face. On the instant, with the two of them standing side by side, Slocum recognized the resemblance. Both boasted handsome, lean features, with bushy eyebrows surmounting pale blue eyes. Only the sheriff was visibly older, at least ten years up on Porter.

"This is no joke, Ty. That saddle-tramp bastard is ruining everything! We've got to catch him, somebody's got to!"

"Okay, little brother."

"Brother?" asked Packer mystified.

"Use your fuckin' eyes, Jay. Can't you see they're goddamn blood brothers? You got tin around your asshole, man? Don't you feel it when you're being screwed?"

"Outside, Porter," said the sheriff. "I got an idea. You two boys stay right where you are. We'll be right back," he added, grinning.

They left and Slocum sat back down on the cot. "Well if this ain't a boot fulla scorpion, I'll be goddamned for a wet-eared drummer boy! Those two sons o' bitches got us dead to rights, man!"

"They got shit!" snapped Packer. "We didn't steal his damned envelope."

" 'Course not, but we're all he's got left in hand. Shit, just to get even for us letting Turnbull fuck things up he'll probably talk that tin-badge brother o' his into hanging us!"

"He wouldn't no such thing."

"Then what in hell is he holding us for, to keep him company? No sir, he's got something nasty boiling up on the back burner for you and me. Just you watch."

The Fairchilds came back, Porter obviously calmer. He produced a $20 gold piece, displaying it between thumb and forefinger.

"Boys, I'm going to flip this coin. You, Slocum, are going to be heads. Packer, you're tails."

"That's me everytime."

"Whoever comes up will get ten days to run out, find your friend and get that envelope back here into my waiting hands. Shoot him if you have to, but I want all forty of those certificates back. With not so much as a dog-eared corner on any one. Understand?"

"Yeah, yeah." Slocum sighed in exasperation.

"Now if you don't get back here in ten days, whichever lucky one is left behind will get himself a rope."

"You'd murder a man in cold blood?" Slocum asked.

"No need for murder, John. Once word gets out that you three stole close to twenty-two thousand dollars along with those stocks, the life savings of practically everybody in this town—"

"You'll get yourself lynched so fast the damned rope'll burn your gullet!" concluded the sheriff, laughing.

"You bastards," said Packer. "You stole twenty-two thousand bucks and the envelope with the stocks was only to cover up. You stole the money earlier, didn't you?"

"No need to get into that," said Fairchild quietly. "It's water over the dam."

"You prick," Slocum said. "You soft-talking, smiling, sneaky son of a bitch! You'd actually make one of us poor bastards kick air just to protect your scaly hide?"

"To say nothing of my reputation. Time's wasting, gentlemen. Heads Slocum, tails Packer."

The coin spun briefly and came down on the back of his left hand. Covering it with his right, he slowly drew his hand away.

"Slocum goes, Packer stays. Unlock the door, Ty."

7

Slocum rode into the storm, heading west for Seminole. He knew Turnbull had a good three-hour headstart and, with the envelope in his saddlebag, all the encouragement he needed to thread together one good string of country miles before sunup on the way to Seminole, where his banker brother-in-law waited.

Astride his stout-chested, strong-backed quarterhorse, Slocum followed the wire-straight mud slough that passed for a road over the border into Earth County in the direction of Dublin. A clutch of shanties spread along both sides of the way.

He was familiar with the state of Texas, almost entirely, save for the Gulf Coast. He'd been through Seminole, although he'd never hung up hat and saddle there. To his recollection it was bigger than Dublin, bigger than Goodnight and Prayerville combined. Locating a man who can fairly well figure he's being tailed promised no easy chore. If he were Turnbull, he'd haul up just outside Seminole, flatten behind a creosote bush, wait for his pursuer to show his unshaven face and bushwhack him deader than last year's Christmas bird.

The road he was riding was the only way into the damned town from the east. He might do better and save his hide in the process, wide-circling and coming down from the north. Or up from the south. He could hole up in some four-bit hotel across the street from the bank, peel his eyes for sight of good old Race and wait. Which presented one more problem. Would the bastard show up at the bank? Why bother? Being brother-in-law kin, he could go to the house instead. Both slyer and safer.

As far as that went, how could he be absolutely certain Turnbull was heading for Seminole in the first place? He could be running for the border. Still, considering the situation in all its dimensions, the bastard had to be hell-bent for his sister's place. Who else but his banker brother-in-law could he count on to turn the stolen paper into hard cash. Would he stick his neck out that far for Turnbull? Slocum couldn't begin to guess. But Turnbull knew the man a lot better than he did.

Screw Turnbull and his damned relatives! Better he think about poor old Jay Packer. He had ten days to get his hands on that envelope and get it back to Fairchild. Which was possible, anything was possible, even Fairchild double-crossing the two of them once he got his certificates back. There was still the matter of the twenty-two thousand cash. It was long gone and somebody would have to take the blame for that. Who better than Fairchild's two favorite bag-holders? Christ Almighty, he could actually fetch back the envelope intact only to come up against a brand new buzz saw!

All the same, he couldn't desert old Jay, never, not even to save himself. Nobody but a four-square prick would let a friend down like that. Poor helpless bastard, sitting in Tyson Fairchild's crummy cell waiting, hoping, wondering, his fingers going to his neck every so often and a lumpy swallow riding down his throat. What really killed the chicken, though, as much as the fix they were in and the deadly consequences threatening, was knowing he himself had been so dead set against joining up with Porter Fairchild in the first place. Every voice in his body, his heart, his conscience, his experience, his common sense had joined in a chorus warning him to stay away. He just wouldn't listen. When did he ever?

Yeah, fuck it, let's do it. Only because I'm sick to death o' living broke, sunk down to dollar whores and stuck in this piss-hole town!

"You dumb bastard, Slocum! You mule-ass fuckhead!"

An armadillo trundled across the road, spooking the horse. Raising his forehooves, the horse pawed the storm and whinnied, and the crossbound stranger vanished into the ditch.

The rain let up shortly before dawn. The sun, as white as a dead man's eye, lifted free of the horizon stretching over the southbound Brazos at Slocum's back. Slipping off his poncho, he shook the water out of it, rolled it up and tied it behind his saddle. He could do with a cup of coffee, he thought—scalding hot, mud brown and thick enough to float a fistful of nails in. And a biscuit or two would sit his gut right comfortably. But everything in all directions gleamed soaking wet from the downpour, including the dead hickory and ash branches scattered along both sides of the road. There could be no coffee fire under such conditions.

The next town would be De Leon, something like 20 soggy miles ahead. He would stop for 15 minutes, rest the horse, uncinch the saddle and let a little air get at his belly and back sweat, give him water and catch a bite to eat himself. No more than 15 minutes, though. He had a nagging feeling that in spite of his hard riding all night he hadn't done much catching up on Turnbull. He wouldn't put it past the bastard to ride his horse into the red ground, trade it for another—tossing his ten bucks into the deal—and take off at a gallop.

He himself would continue riding at a steady gait. If he failed to catch up before Seminole, so be it. Facing the bastard down so beat he could hardly keep his eyes open made no sense at all.

He rode on toward midday between long-needled pine separated by impenetrable thickets of hawthorn and holly interspersed with the white- purple- and gray-barked giant plane trees.

He encountered no one, no white man, no Indian, indeed few living creatures apart from quail, a single spotted skunk and turkey buzzards spreading their frayed-looking wings black against the dazzling dying sun. De Leon came and went. He rode on, thinking of Jay Packer. Little Jay, no more than five feet, seven inches standing on new-tapped boot heels, built like a seven-hooped oil barrel, his upper arms so big around Slocum couldn't fit his thumbs and index fingers about them. He'd tried. A whiskey nose balanced between flashing green eyes—eyes filled with fire and brimstone, especially when the man using them got half a bottle of rotgut inside his skin.

The two of them had had some wild times together in the gray army, with the good ol' boys. He'd seen Red-Fur Packer clean up three and four smart alecks at a time, one-punching them flat, redistributing their teeth in their faces, unhooking their jaws, pushing their belly buttons flush against their spines and upsetting the surrounding organs in quite the way a horse kick in the gut upsets.

In five years in uniform Jay Packer had spent more time behind bars than in front of them, all of it for fighting. And nearly every time taking on his fellow graybacks in the platoon, the squad, the company, the regiment. He never had been overly particular. For anybody spoiling to bleed he was ready. If they didn't want to, he was ready, too. A grin creased Slocum's stubbled features. He'd never forget the day Colonel Fatass Severns called the two of them on the carpet for assaulting a bunch of idiot noncoms. He'd announced that Private Packer—loyal defender of the Confederacy though he'd proven himself, courageous, able and all the rest of it—was tougher on his own damned regiment, broke more bones, liberated more blood, distributed more teeth and effected more property damage, personal and governmental, "than any troop of blue bellies this outfit has ever come up against!"

"Who the hell's sahd is yo-all on, private? Yoh a gawd-damned menace to the Cawn-fedracee, that's what y'are. I gawt a mind to chain yo-all up in a gawd-damned tree 'til the gawd-damned wah is ovah!"

But what a soldier that Red Fur was—rifle, bayonet, hand-to-hand. Nothing or no one could back him down. Slocum's thoughts went back to the Goodnight jail cell and his and Packer's parting words.

"Bring that son of a bitch's head back in your saddlebag, will you, John?"

"Screw him. All I'm lookin' to bring back are those damned certificates."

"Them, too. But bring his head back for me."

"What in hell for?"

"So's I can knock his goddamn teeth out!"

"You're crazier than a Mex bedbug, you know that?"

"So they tell me. Take care o' your ass, tall boy. How you expect to pull it off without me backin' you up beats me. Just don't let him shoot your dick off. You can bet he knows you're comin'."

"He's got to be dumber than you are not to."

"And you'll be goin' through the heart o' Nermernuh country. They get their greasy paws on you and they'll chop you up for dog meat."

"I ain't afraid o' no Comanche. I've bullshitted 'em before, I'll bullshit 'em again."

"There's allus a last time with them bastards. Whatever happens, if they yell you down, don't try to outride 'em. Palaver, talk nice as apple pie to 'em, give 'em anything they fancy, including your asshole, and they'll leave you intact."

"They won't fuck with me, friend. They ain't near as nasty as they used to be back before the hostilities."

"Be sure you remind 'em of that when they back you up to a tree and decide to use you for a pincushion."

"Any more advice, Red Father?"

"Yeah, see you get back here in ten days, or you'll need a goddamned shovel to see this handsome face again."

"I know, I know."

They had shaken hands, and impulsively Jay had thrown his arms around Slocum's shoulders, hugging him briefly, patting his back hard with both hands. It gave John a decidedly uncomfortable feeling. Putting one's own hide on the line was one thing, but when one of the best friends you'd ever made is counting on you, when his life is placed squarely in your hands, that proved out something else, something close to scary. At that moment, as at this, he wished with all his heart the damned business was over—Turnbull out of the picture, dead or close enough to it to regret his actions, the stock certificates returned to Fairchild and he and Packer back on the trail for Eagle Pass.

He stopped off in De Leon as planned and was back on the trail shortly. He was heading straight into more rain cascading down from a bulge-bellied cloud overhead, pounding the brim of his Stetson and his horse's flanks. The muddy road turned into a narrow quagmire, slowing the pace considerably. Still, he decided, there was no point in waiting out the storm. Better he try and outrun it. The rain collected in the curl of his brim and ran out the break at the back, spilling down onto his poncho in a steady stream. It was close to three in the afternoon, but from the condition of the sky and the dark desolation stretching to the dimly visible horizon one would have guessed it was the middle of the night. Coming to a caved-in bridge, he was forced to follow the rain-angered stream a half mile off his route before he found a fordable spot.

The downpour flailed the countryside, battering horse and rider with abandon. It continued for three hours before a death-like blue-whiteness blanketed the world of the Comanchería. He could feel his horse tiring, fighting the mud underhoof, the strain telling on his lungs, his breath clouding forth in short bursts, his lips lathering. Riding him through another night was out of the question. He couldn't do that to any horse much less this hard-working 1200 pounds of good-natured cattle pusher.

Stopping and letting the animal graze by the side of the road, he made a supper of dry biscuit and beef jerky picked up on his stopover in De Leon. Then he bedded down for the night, his head against his saddle, his poncho stretched over his blanket in case of a sudden return of the rain. The sky had cleared, however, a quarter moon hanging low in the west, stars twinkling around it as if it were a heavenly corral. The night air was pleasantly mild for that late in the year. It tasted clean after the rain and smelled of pine. He fell asleep at once, his .44 unleathered in his right hand under the blanket and poncho. The last sight to meet his eyes was that of his horse contentedly nibbling the glistening grass within six feet of the road.

The first sight to meet his eyes upon awakening was decidedly less tranquil. A face—homely, copper-hued, deeply wrinkled, with great valleys and clefts under the cheekbones, across the chin and laddering the neck—gathered around glinting black eyes and a corrugated forehead. Atop the face the hair was iron-gray, pulled down both sides into braids wound with otter fur and decorated with beadwork. Short lanyards hung from the top of his head and a daisy pendant decorated the scrotum-like flesh at his throat. And in the center of this collective ugliness so loosely attached to the skull behind it was a nose like a putty ball. Slocum would have laughed out loud but for the braves gripping hunting lances and rifles standing around the old man.

Slocum's first impulse was to tighten his grip on the .44 concealed beneath his covers. He was about to bring it up—blanket, poncho and all—and jam it against the old man's chicken chest, when he changed his mind. Jamming the gun back into his holster, he leaped to his feet.

"Okay, everybody mount up!" he yelled, gesturing authoritatively. "Shake it up, let's go! We're moving out!" Bending, he rolled up his blanket and poncho, tucking them under one arm. Confusion flooded the faces before him. And the most bewildered look of all belonged to Putty Nose. But in spite of Slocum's loud and demanding tone and his vigorous gesturing, nobody moved a moccasin.

"All right, who savvys English? Speak up, come on!"

Six feet of brave, tall for a Comanche, pushed forward. "Me, Tonowa, speak white-man's tongue."

"Okay, Tonowa, you take me to your chief. I mean pronto, fast as we can get there. Chief?"

"White Fox."

"Right. We got to powwow, him and me. Everybody, let's go! We got no time to lose!" Snatching up his saddle he forced his way past the old man and through the semicircle, running toward his horse. "Come on! Come on!"

The instant he turned his back on them, the top half of his spine took a lance, in imagination, thrown so hard it pierced his body. So real was the feel he grit his teeth, hunched his shoulders and broke out in a heavy sweat. It hurt like hell, like a calf iron jammed through. No, not that much, it couldn't possibly. It was too fast into him. In two seconds he'd be dead. Maybe time for one surge of agonizing pain, one goodbye scream, then down he'd go like a well-felled tree. As dead as the stump it leaves.

He sighed inwardly fit to stretch his windpipe when no lance arrived. He could hear them jabbering loudly. Reaching his horse, he flung the saddle over its back and turned.

"I'm telling you move! Now! Let's go!"

As if a hornet's nest had dropped into their midst, they sprang to action, racing to their ponies, leaping lightly onto them and heeling away at top speed. By this time, Slocum had cinched up. His roll and poncho still tucked under one arm, he rode out into their midst, digging his spurs deep, pushing his horse through the group and into the lead beside Tonowa. Throwing a glance back over his right shoulder he urged them forward.

"Come on! Faster, faster!"

They rode a good two miles in a northwesterly direction, the old man falling well back of the pack before they had covered half the distance. Spattering mud in every direction they rushed across open country, up a gentle grade and down through a narrow arroyo. Slocum's mind was spinning, silently going over his speech to come. Loose shale clattered under hooves. The sound bounced off the sheer walls of the passage, setting up an earsplitting din. Then, two by two, Tonowa and Slocum still in the lead, they emerged onto a scrub-littered plain.

It was working beautifully, reflected Slocum, too perfectly to believe. Lying there with the nape of his neck against his saddle, his hand gripping his .44 under the blanket, he had awakened to three options: shoot Putty Nose and make a stand with five shots left against 12 well-armed men; surrender immediately, cooperate and pray his head and his scalp would still be joined come sunup, or turn the tables on the bastards.

What white man ever jumped up out of a sound sleep, holstered his six-gun and began demanding a whole hunting party of Comanches to mount up and get him to their chief as fast as they could? No white man in his right mind, perhaps, but Slocum was aware from long experience that the only way to bamboozle a redskin was to pull the unexpected, knock his thinking off balance and keep it there.

And so far it was working.

Dawn was creeping over the ridge of hills lacing the Edwards Plateau to the east as they came within sight of camp. Mild weather encouraged the tribe to tangle together brush arbors for homes and to sleep on light bedding under the stars. Only one tepee—20 buffalo skins joined and fitted over the customary 22 cedar poles, properly flapped and ditched—occupied the area. Its smokehole puffed slender plumes skyward. White Fox's palatial residence, mused Slocum. It had to be. Squaws in greasy-beaded buckskins were up and at their pots, stewing buffalo paunches, stinking up the air. The Nermernuh, Slocum knew, never washed, from his first breath into the world to his dying one. They would mess up a site until the stench from rotten meat, human feces, body odor and sundry other things commingling became unbearable. Only then would they move on. The squaws squatting at their fires jabbered raucously and naked children sat about playing with stones and munching Comanche candy—mesquite beans combined with buffalo bone marrow and pemmican.*

Slocum and the others hurtled into camp, jumped down and scattered. John ran a line straight to the tepee. Knowing the Comanche's ways and his mind, he was confident that nobody, least of all a white man, ever

---

******dried meat strips flavored with crushed nuts, fruits, or berries* barged into a Comanche chief's tepee without escort or unannounced. Such boldness was unheard of. But under the circumstances it was the best possible play he could make, serving as it would to underscore the pretended vital importance of his mission, the desperate necessity for utmost speed in taking action once he broke the news.

Shaking Tonowa's hand off his shoulder, he pushed through the flap, interrupting White Fox and his *puhakut* in discussion.

The air inside the tepee was so malodorous, so nauseating he almost gagged out loud. But he held his throat in check and planting himself directly before the chief addressed him in somber tones. Again shaking off Tonowa's grip on his shoulder.

"Chief White Fox, I have come from the Great White Chief with news of death and destruction!"

From the look on Tonowa's face he was patently embarrassed by his failure to keep Pale-eyes from intruding. But he obligingly launched into translation.

"What death? What destruction?" asked the wizened little *puhakut* in perfect English, narrowing his eyes suspiciously.

Slocum assumed a face of grievously grave concern and explained. The Comanche, he knew, was the most skillful horseman in the world. At 30 feet he could drive an arrow clean through a full-grown bull buffalo. He could do likewise one-handing a rifle at full gallop. He wasn't as tall as the Cheyenne nor as short as the Pima, but name the three best fighting men out of all the tribes and clans and countries between both poles, and one of the three had to be a Comanche. For sheer ability, resourcefulness and courage under fire no man born could outperform the Nermernuh.

And his character was widely known. His most treasured possession hung beside his medicine bag between his legs. His gods were protective spirits who dwelt in rocks, in the thunder and in animals. His religion had no ethic or concept of moral uplifting, no notion of reward or punishment. He listened to his *shaman-puhakut,* he treated his dog and his horse better than his females and he lived with power and died with honor.

He had only one weakness, that which afflicted every tribe from the Chinooks of Oregon to the Seminoles in Florida, from the Penobscots in Maine to the tall Yumas of lower California. He was superstitious. Ghosts imbued all Indians with uneasiness, including the Comanche. His ghost image was of skeletons that rose with the moon and scalped, blood-covered specters who walked in darkness. He believed also in the *nenuh-pee,* man-like creatures only a foot tall capable of shooting arrows that never failed to kill.

But his greatest fear was reserved for a creature of his own devising, a monster recognized only by the Nermernuh.

Kneeling with his back to White Fox, who looked enough like Putty Nose to be his brother and doubtless was, and the little *puhakut,* Slocum quickly sketched the outline of an owl in the sand. Under it he added a number of round-cornered bones similar to the cross-bones on the Jolly Roger. Moving out of the chief's line of sight, he stood up. The owl's likeness was no better, perhaps, not as good as that which a six-year-old with one eye might draw. Nevertheless it could hardly be mistaken for a horse or buffalo. White Fox took one look and gasped—long, loudly and deep in his throat—the death rattle of a man very much alive. His *puhakut* also reacted fearfully.

"Yes, brave chief. The Cannibal Owl, the monster that descends in darkness to devour men. Who swallows buffalo whole and spits the bones over the Great Plains. I bring you warning of the coming of the Cannibal Owl."

Ignoring Slocum for a moment, White Fox began talking with his *puhakut,* the two of them plainly shaken. And Tonowa no less visibly upset.

"You have seen the Cannibal Owl?" inquired the *puhakut.*

Slocum nodded soberly. He pointed past them. "In the west. The Great White Chief has sent many blue soldiers to find and destroy it."

"The Cannibal Owl cannot be destroyed," said the *puhakut.* "It was born fully grown of a stone egg and will live forever. Fire arrows, bullets smeared with blood, poisoned lances cannot harm it."

"The blue soldiers have a plan," said Slocum.

White Fox spoke briefly.

"White Fox ask what they are doing?" the *puhakut* said.

"First they tried to catch it in a net made of strong wire." He gripped his wrist. "So thick. And big, big as twenty-five Comanche blankets sewn together. They tried to drop the net over it from a cliff. But with its claws of iron it ripped the net like a straw basket.

"Now they plan to lure the Cannibal Owl into a ravine, block its way and push heavy stones down upon it. Crush it."

The *puhakut* shook his head as he interrupted. "That has been tried before. With its great wings that beat like thunder the Cannibal Owl will shake off the biggest stones. The monster cannot be killed, cannot die!"

"Chief White Fox, I bring word from the Great White Chief that you and your people must move your camp as soon as you can. It stands in the path of the Cannibal Owl. Two moons, three at most, the monster will be coming through here." He pointed east. "You can move into the daylight to one side or the other out of its way, up the Great Plains or down to the Stockton Plateau. Anywhere but into the night." He pointed westward dramatically. "From there it is coming, into the heart of the Comanchería. You must pick up and leave!"

The *puhakut* nodded. "Pale-eyes speaks wisdom. We will do well to heed his words."

Good boy, thought Slocum, sell the greasy son of a bitch. White Fox needed little persuading. His head bobbed up and down vigorously in agreement. Slocum cleared his throat.

"I go now."

"You stay!" snapped the *puhakut*.

Slocum tensed, fighting down the nervousness in his stomach, shaking his head. "I go. The other *rancherías* must be warned. The path of the Cannibal Owl must be cleared. What chiefs are closest to you?"

"Lone Dog and the Cut Cheeks are one moon's ride toward the Stockton Plateau," said the *puhakut*. Tonowa nodded.

"That's bad," said Slocum worriedly. "I'll have to get down there right away. You, great chief, get your people started. Time is very short."

Raising his hand in salute, he ducked out of the tepee and mounted up. White Fox, the *puhakut* and Tonowa looked on at the tepee flap. And every brave, squaw and child stood frozen, staring.

Out he rode at a gallop.

8

The rain rattled the roof of the dilapidated stable like 20 drums in unison sounding assembly. The drab interior was as dark and gloomy as night, thanks to the storm. It was cluttered with tools and equipment and the moisture-laden air was heavy with the stink of fresh horseshit. Slocum shook his shoulders, freeing his poncho of the wet, as the old man hoisted his Buckeye Tubular lamp and surveyed the horse with one good eye.

"I seed worn-out horseflesh afore, but this fella looks like he climbed up outta his own grave. Look at that mud, will you!"

"We come a long way, mister."

"Alasker?"

Slocum managed a tired smile. "Brush him down,

give him oats if you got any and let him drink to his heart's content."

"You're the boss."

The old man's glance lit on the saddle and he ran the tips of his fingers down the horn stitching admiringly. "Some good-looking seat, you got there. Wouldn't wanta sell it, would you?"

"Nope. Is it okay if I leave my rifle in the boot?"

"Sure, it's safe enough here. How long you figure to lay over?"

"Two or three days."

"Where'll you be stayin'?"

"Got any ideas?"

"You might try the Bluebonnet House just up the street. The rooms is only fifty cents a night. No cockroaches, so they say, and the rats ain't overly troublesome."

"The Bluebonnet House." Slocum handed him a dollar. "On account. Take good care of him, he's one good horse. Be seeing you." He started for the door, stopped and turned. "By the way, you see anything of a stranger in town? Big man, big shoulders, blond hair that looks like wet hay, long pointy blond oxbow mustache sticking out both sides? He'd be riding a sorry-looking sorrel with a white line down the center of its face."

The old man scratched his chin and shook his head slowly. "Nope, can't say I seen anybody like that."

The lobby of the Bluebonnet House was crowded with the Seminoleans who preferred a comfortable chair, the civilized stink of cigar smoke, idle conversation and seconds on somebody else's newspaper to the dismal weather outside. Slocum was handed a key to a room on the second floor located at the front. From either of his two windows he was able to look out across and up the street four doors to the Gaines County Citizens Bank, resplendent in a fresh coat of paint, its sign proclaiming its assets to be "over $60,000." At first sight of it Slocum wondered if that figure included the value of certain Southern Pacific–Texas and Pacific Railroad stock recently come to town.

He scraped away five days' beard and washed up at the open window, his eyes glued to the bank, his worries mounting. Assuming Turnbull had shown up in town, what if he'd already made his deal with his brother-in-law? Even, God forbid, already pulled out? That would really screw up the works.

What he ought to be doing was tracking down the double-crossing prick, pinpointing his sister's house and keeping an eye on *it* instead of the damned bank. At least that way he'd stand a chance of getting the drop on Turnbull.

As if worrying about the whereabouts of the certificates wasn't enough, there was Goodnight rooting itself in the back of his mind like a patch of poison jimsonweed. If he did get lucky, more than lucky, if lightning struck and one way or another he was able to get his hands on the stocks, how would he work the Goodnight end of the deal with the Fairchilds?

He certainly couldn't ride into town waving the damned things overhead demanding Jay Packer's release. No, better he stop off a couple miles this side of Goodnight, bury all but one of the certificates, ride on in, show the certificate to them, order Packer's release, get his ass on the road and two hours out of town, then tell the two bastards where he'd buried the remainder of the stocks. If necessary, he'd ride out there with them, then take off and catch up with Packer at some prearranged spot. At least that way there was a chance of the two of them getting clear of the area alive.

But the more he thought about it, the more he became convinced that Porter Fairchild had no intention of letting either of them get away. He and his tin-badge brother would breathe a lot easier once they'd turned him and Jay over to Goodnight's irate bank depositors. Once the Fairchilds let the story out that three drifters had busted into the bank and stolen the people's hard-earned cash, he and Jay would be ripe for lynching.

Still the big problem—getting Packer and himself out of the Goodnight stewpot—would be no problem at all if he didn't find a solution to the problem at hand. And he wasn't doing much in that direction sitting by a damned window staring down at the Gaines County Citizens Bank watching Seminole citizens pass in and out the big double doors. The rain had stopped and the sun came out in the middle of the afternoon. This served to increase the flow of traffic below. The sun filling the puddles with gold was a pleasant sight, but the longer Slocum sat at the window staring the more fidgety he became.

He had to start some kind of ball rolling. He couldn't just sit there like a potted plant for the next three days. Tomorrow would be the fourth of the ten days, and before he knew it his waiting would be eating so deeply into that limit that even if he did get his hands on the stocks he wouldn't be able to get back to Goodnight in time to save Packer's neck. As risky as it might be, he'd have to start making inquiries. Better yet, slip the old man down at the stable an extra dollar and send him wandering around town asking after Race Turnbull.

If only he knew what the bastard's brother-in-law looked like. He could safely assume that by now the stocks had changed hands. Turnbull had to have beaten him into town, and, once arrived, he'd dump the paper in two shakes. Which meant the banker would be the one to look for.

While Slocum looked on, a dozen well-dressed types entered and left the bank, anyone of whom could have been Turnbull's brother-in-law. Then suddenly, Slocum got his first real break. The great God Luck, seated on his golden cloud casting an appraising eye over the world, fixing on North America, on Texas, on Gaines County, on Seminole, on the window of room 2B in the Bluebonnet House, winked at John Slocum. Slocum's heart jumped clear up into his throat as he caught sight of a rugged little Indian pony coming down the street, a familiar figure astride it. His Stetson pulled well down over his eyes, Race Turnbull nevertheless betrayed his identity by the two blond points of mustache thrusting straight out either side. The broadness and self-conscious hunch of his shoulders, the studded metal Ts for Turnbull on the backs of his gloves and the oversized rowels on his spurs confirmed it.

Slocum watched in fascination as he rode straight up to the Bluebonnet House, dismounted and came into the hotel. Rushing to his door, John opened just wide enough to enable him to see over the railing into the crowded lobby below. Turnbull marched into view, his saddlebags over one shoulder. He stopped at the desk, got his room key from the slender, dough-faced little corpse of a clerk and started jauntily up the winding staircase, whistling loudly as he came.

Slocum ducked back inside, closing the door. He could hear him reach the landing still whistling, unlock the door of 2A on the other side of the wall, enter and bolt the door behind him.

Slocum glanced at the well-stained heavy pier mirror above his washstand, grinning like a lunatic. "Will you look at you, mister! You've just won yourself the big pot with four pretty little aces!"

What a break! Wasn't that luck's way, though, he mused. Running through your days stinking, black and rotten for interminable lengths of time, then suddenly swinging about and exploding in your face, showering you with liquid gold! Answering a prayer never even uttered, because you recognized the patent uselessness of asking the impossible.

This was it. Checking his .44, he releathered it, slapped it for luck and walked the short way down to the new arrival's room. He tapped the door.

"Yeah?" asked Turnbull.

Slocum covered his mouth with one hand and talked into it. "Message, Mr. Turnbull."

"Stick it under the door."

Shit! "Telegram, sir, you got to sign."

"I'll sign later, stick it under the door."

Slocum hesitated, backed against the railing, lifted his right boot high and slammed full force against the knob. The door snapped open with a loud splintering sound. Turnbull was standing over the bed, his saddlebags in one hand, his .45 in the other, bringing it up and firing. The bullet grazed the door jamb, whitening it.

At the same instant Slocum fired, catching him in the shoulder, spinning him about. Slocum's second shot hit him flush in the kidney. Turnbull doubled over with a loud groan, his head smashing against the windowsill. He toppled over dead.

Slocum snatched up the saddlebags, ran past the body and was out the open window and onto the narrow walkway in five seconds. Crouching low, moving swiftly down to his own open window, he dropped down into the room, closing and locking the window. Tossing the saddlebags onto the bed he searched them quickly, his hands trembling.

Both were empty.

9

Cursing loudly, Slocum slammed the empty bags onto the bed. Then he froze as he heard loud voices and running, people coming up the stairs, milling about on the landing. Unbuckling his gunbelt, he lifted the mattress and spread his belt, holster, .44 and all underneath. Placing the saddlebags also, he let the mattress drop back down into place.

He was getting ready to go outside and join the crowd when his eyes wandered to the bank below. A tall good-looking middle-aged man wearing a fancy worsted suit and nutria-fur fedora came out of the bank carrying a satchel. He came straight toward the hotel.

Turning from the window, Slocum went to the door and opened it. At least 20 men and women were crowding around the door to Turnbull's room, those nearest Slocum with their backs to him. He eased up behind them, pushing toward Turnbull's door, glancing down into the lobby just as the well-dressed satchel-carrier came in and started up the stairs.

Halfway to the landing the stranger stopped and asked a man passing him on the way down what all the hubbub was about. Slocum could not make out the explanation, but the man with the satchel understood perfectly. Paling, he cast about like a cornered dog, looked down at the bag in his hand, then quickly turned and vanished out the front door.

Retreating into his room, Slocum watched him pick his way through the mud back to the bank.

Turnbull's brother-in-law! It had to be. It all fit neat as knots in a board, Turnbull bringing his empty saddlebags up to his room, what for but to put the money in he was getting for the stocks? What he'd obviously done was given them over as soon as he'd gotten to town. Giving his brother-in-law time to check out their authenticity and value and scrape up payment. After all, it wasn't the sort of savory transaction any banker with a brain between his ears would elect to carry out at his bank. Why take unnecessary chances? Turnbull had to be acting on his brother-in-law's instructions. But when the banker was told that the man in 2A had been killed, that ended things on the spot.

All of which was very interesting but appeared to leave Slocum right back where he'd started—suddenly called upon to rob a bank.

10

Slocum didn't much like the idea of having to rob the bank to get those stocks. Once a safe was blown you had to move six times faster than a jackrabbit if you wanted to get out of the place alive. It was usually close and scary and not nearly as much fun as the James boys and certain other brag mouths made it out to be.

And the only thing worse than robbing a bank in the company of friends was doing it all by your lonesome.

Nevertheless, all logic and common sense persuaded Slocum that the red envelope with the string around it, containing the stocks, had to be sitting in the safe across the street. And since there appeared scant possibility that Turnbull's brother-in-law figured to hand the envelope over to him upon polite request, his only recourse would be to open the safe and take it.

The afternoon shadows were lengthening, the street below rapidly drying up and the bank closing for the day, when Slocum made the only decision he could make. He would buy the necessary dynamite at the general store, hang around the Bluebonnet House until midnight, fetch his horse from the stable, tie him out back of the bank and go to work.

If something went wrong, if he got caught, they'd toss him in a cell, turn the key in the lock and hang poor old Jay Packer 300-odd miles away. And he himself could end up in State Prison in Huntsville or Rusk doing five to ten for engaging in bank business after hours. He was preparing to go out shopping when a knock came at the door. He opened it to the sight of two tin badges with a sheriff and his overgrown deputy attached to them.

"Mr.—"

"Slocum," said John. "Come in."

The sheriff sat down on the edge of the bed, his cheeks less than two inches from the lump created by Slocum's .44 under the mattress. The deputy, all six feet, five inches of him, took his stance back against the door, legs spread, arms folded.

"I got a few questions for you," said the sheriff, fixing his stone-gray eyes on Slocum in silent expectation of honest answers.

"Fire away," said Slocum.

"Were you in your room here when the fellow next door got gunned down this afternoon?"

"Yup. Lying on my bed there resting."

"Your door was closed?"
"Yup."
"So you didn't see anybody."
"Nope."
"Did you hear anything?"
"I was half asleep so I didn't hear anybody come up the stairs or down the hall. The first thing I did hear was somebody shouldering in his door. Then a shot that sounded a little bit like two at once, you know what I mean, that loud. Then another shot, feet scrambling and somebody running by my door. By the time I got up to look, there was nobody there."
"Show us." As soon as the sheriff got up, the deputy got out of the way. Slocum opened the door and pointed down the hall to the open window at the end overlooking a narrow alley.
"Are you saying you saw somebody go out that window?" the sheriff asked, testing him.
"I already said. I didn't *see* anything, I heard."
"It's a good twenty feet down and hardpan below," said the deputy. "Anybody who dropped out that window could break a leg easy."
The sheriff thought a moment, pursing his lips and squinting his brain into gear. "It's still possible, Sam. Mr. Slocum, you're sure you heard somebody run by?"
"Sure as we're standing here. Sounded like half a horse."
They went back into the room, the deputy resuming his stance at the door.
"Where do you hail from, Mr. Slocum?" asked the sheriff.
"I'm down from Kansas City on my way to Mexico."
"For what?"
"Any job I can get."
"What were you doing up in Kansas City?"
"Freighting."
"You looking for the same thing down Mexico way?"
"Nope. Buddy o' mine in Nogales is starting up a cattle spread. He's looking for help."

"How come you stopped over in Seminole?"
"To rest my horse. And my butt."
"How long you fixin' to stay?"
"Couple days."
"Did you happen to know the fellow next door?"
"I never laid eyes on him. I just got to town this afternoon. Haven't even set foot out that door."
"So you never even saw his face."
"Nope."
"Do you carry a gun?"
"Just a rifle."
"No handgun?"
"Nope."
"That's a little strange, ain't it? You're traveling all the way from Kansas City down to Nogales without protection?"
"My rifle's protection enough. On the trail it's a sight better than any pistol."
"Mind if I have a look at it?"
"Feel free. It's down to the stable with my horse. I got no need for firearms when I'm in a town. My feelings is them that carries 'em is asking for trouble."
"That's interesting. Sam and me wish a lotta folks felt the same way, ain't that right, Sam?"
Sam stared at Slocum. "It sounds fishy as hell to me, Bob."
"I don't give a plateful o' shit how it sounds, soldier!" snapped Slocum heatedly.
"Easy does it," the sheriff said.
"Like I told you, my rifle's down to the stable. What was it killed the fella next door?"
"Doc Frydenborg dug a .44 slug outta his back."
"My rifle's a 30-06 Winchester."
"A nice piece. Okay, I guess that does it for now. But do us a small favor, will you?"
"If I can."
"Stop and check at the office before you leave town, okay?"
"Will do."

They left, Slocum closing the door, letting out a seven-second sigh and slumping down into his chair by the window. It didn't appear too messy, he decided. If they suspected him, the sheriff especially was doing a great job of concealing it. The only bone in the soup was his goddamn .44! The old man at the stable had to have seen him wearing it when he took the dollar out of his pocket, lifting his arm and with it his poncho. Not so with the desk clerk, though. He'd stood belly up to the desk and there was no way he could have seen the gun when Slocum reached up to accept his room key.

Thank the good Lord for the rain and the poncho. All the same, knowing the law, they'd be back. They certainly weren't interested in his rifle. The first question they'd ask at the stable had to be "Was he wearing a pistol?" The old man's answer could be I don't know, could be, I don't recollect noticing, or "yes." Most likely the last.

But there was even a hairier possibility than that. The old man might very well recall that he, Slocum, had described Turnbull, mustache and all. If the conversation got around to that, the sheriff and his overgrown sidekick would be back with wheels on their heels!

Life certainly seemed to be getting tedious.

11

Either the sheriff and his deputy were too busy following up rumors regarding Turnbull's demise, or they hadn't gotten around to or couldn't be bothered questioning the old man. Whatever the case, Slocum saw no more of either of them the rest of the day. He bought three sticks of Pritchard dynamite and fuse at the store and picked up his horse.

Under a crescent moon in a setting of twinkling blue stars he tied up at the rear of the bank, kicked in the alley door and barged in—.44 in one hand, dynamite in the other and two matches in his teeth.

The bank was half again the size of the Goodnight bank, the interior entirely different. Two small offices occupied the two rear corners, no safe could be seen, and the tellers' stations at the front were set up against one long two-foot-high cross-woven steel cage, instead of the usual individual cages. A lamp was visible through the glass upper half of one of the office doors. The instant Slocum entered, the door opened part way and a man stuck his head out. He licked his lips and swallowed hard at sight of the gun in the intruder's hand. He was, noted Slocum, the man with the satchel. Swearing under his breath, John spat the matches to the floor and confronted him.

"Open it all the way, then raise 'em high."

"Don't shoot. I have a wife and child."

"I ain't gonna shoot nobody. You just do like I tell you and everything'll be roses."

Slocum pushed him back into his office, the muzzle of his gun hard against his vest. He glanced about. A four-foot-high Cincinnati safe on wheels stood in one corner. Slocum waved his gun at it.

"Open up."

"Yes, sir."

"Make it fast."

The man gulped, nodded, knelt and began fumbling with the combination, his hands shaking like a Colorado aspen.

"Calm down, dammit! You ain't gonna get hurt!"

"No, sir. Yes, sir. No, sir."

"Shut up!"

Flexing his fingers and sweating, his hands continued to tremble. He finally got the door open.

"Everything out on the floor!" snapped Slocum. Picking the lamp up from the desk he held it over the man as he emptied the safe. Slocum's heart tugged. There it was, big and red as could be, neatly tied. "That envelope, open it up, quick!"

"It's stocks."

"Shut up. Just do it."

But his hands were shaking so he couldn't manage the knot. Snatching the envelope away from him, Slocum dropped it, placed a foot on it and yanked the string 'til it broke. The stocks were inside.

"What are you doing with these?" he asked coldly.

"One of our depositors—"

"Don't lie to me, you son of a bitch. These are hot and you know it! You got no right holding 'em!"

"I don't understand."

"I'll bet you don't. You bank bastards are all alike, all double-dealing pillars of the community. I oughta kick your ass into two halves. Get up!"

"What are you going to do?"

"What do you want me to do, put six into your yellow belly?"

"I have a wife and child, a little boy."

"And he's got a crook for an old man. When you get home, *if* you get home, tell him. Tell him his old man's a goddamned double-dealing crooked son of a bitch! He's got a right to know!"

Slocum's eyes drifted across the desk as he set the lamp back down. Leaning against a pigeonhole was a deputy's badge. He picked it up, examining it.

"What are you doing with this?"

"I'm a—what you'd call a citizen deputy."

"That's pretty good. You work both sides o' the fence. It must keep you fairly busy hoppin' back and forth." Slocum started to toss down the badge but changed his mind and pocketed it instead. "My souvenir of Seminole. Okay, everything back into the safe except that red envelope. Make it fast."

"How did you know about those stocks?" asked the man in a tremulous voice.

"None o' your goddamned business. Okay, shut the door and spin the combination." The man complied, then rose slowly to his feet. "Let's go," said Slocum.

"Where?"

"Don't ask questions, just move."

12

They double-rode north up the Llano Estacado. The air was soft and warm as a woolly blanket. The stillness was broken only by the murmuring breeze floating down from the craggy heights of the distant Rockies across the New Mexico border and the sound of the overburdened horse's shoes clacking against the loose shale. Now and again a darkened farmhouse revealed itself, nudging upward through the base of the star-studded sky.

Turnbull's brother-in-law rode behind Slocum on the horse's rump, his wrists tied around Slocum's belt buckle. They had ridden close to six miles by Slocum's reckoning when the other man summoned up the dregs of his courage and addressed John:

"Can't you at least tell me where you're taking me?"

"To a real nice spot for starting a long walk."

"We've come at least ten miles already."

"Not even seven."

"Oh."

The shale clacked, the breeze rose and died, the stars glittered ostentatiously.

"I'm curious about one thing—"

"What?" asked Slocum.

"It's none of my business, of course, and you don't have to tell me. But would I be wrong in assuming you were the one who shot Horace?"

"What?" asked Slocum in astonishment.

"Horace Turnbull."

Slocum reined up. "Just hold everything." Untying the man's wrists he ordered him down off the horse, getting down himself. "Are you trying to tell me Race Turnbull's been shot? How bad?"

The man stared, searching Slocum's eyes. "As if you didn't know."

"I don't, damn it! Now talk, tell me!"

The look on the other's face was that of conviction and disbelief. "He was shot and killed this afternoon at the Bluebonnet House."

"And you think I did it?" asked Slocum heatedly. "You're a damned fool! We was in business together, him and me. Partners. Besides which I didn't even get to town 'til after sundown."

"He told me—"

"He told you him and me and another guy stole the stocks from the bank in Goodnight, right?" The man nodded. "On account they was all we could find in the safe. He claimed he had a brother-in-law who'd take 'em off his hands for a nice bundle, at least half the value. He was to give 'em over to you, you pay, he clears out, I steal back the stocks, ride out and join him. Then the two of us go to another town a hundred miles away and pull the same game. It's a damned flimflam, don't you see? The idea is you don't squawk when I rob you on account you got no legal right to be holding the stocks in the first place, get it?"

"I see."

"Do you?"

"Let me put it this way. Knowing Horace, I wouldn't put it past him."

"You paid him, right?"

The man explained why he was unable to. "But if you didn't shoot him, then who did?"

"I'd hardly shoot the damned goose about to lay the gold egg, would I? Besides, like I said, I never got there 'til after sundown." Slocum paused. "Are you sure *you* didn't shoot him? It wouldn't be the first time a man'd try to keep his pie and eat it, too."

"Cake."

"Huh?"

"The idea's ridiculous, I don't even carry a gun. Besides, how could I kill my own wife's brother?"

"Well, old Race had his share o' enemies, all right. It doesn't surprise me none somebody caught up with him."

The man stared at Slocum. John decided he wasn't in the market for any such outlandish bullshit, not half a word of it. Still, there was no harm in trying. He couldn't gun the son of a bitch down. All he could do was turn him loose and let him walk home. Giving himself a decent headstart on the Seminole law. Once over the border into Dawson County he'd be out of old Sheriff Bob's reach anyhow.

But leaving this one believing he knew nothing about Turnbull's being shot had to be worth the effort. Unbuckling his saddlebag, he took out the envelope containing the stocks.

"I don't know what use these are to me now with Race dead," he said resignedly. The banker's eyes lit up, not much, but just enough to betray the greed surging about in his mind.

"Ahem. I never did get to pay Horace, poor chap. What would you say if I were to offer you five thousand for them, cash?"

"They're worth twenty."

"Only to the chap whose name is on them. Five thousand's a fair price."

"And what'll they get you, ten or fifteen?"

He shrugged. "It's hard to tell."

"I'll bet. You double-dealing son of a bitch!"

"Mister, I'm making you a very handsome offer."

"Turn around and start walking."

"Ahem, if you like. Tsk tsk, what a waste. Good evening to you."

He started back the way they had come, stopped, turned and called out. "Seventy-five hundred?" Slocum drew his .44 and pointed it at him. Up came his hands defensively as he backed away. "Okay, okay, we'll forget the whole thing."

13

Cutting southeast, John got back to the road he had followed through the Comanchería from De Leon. Exhausted and unnerved he slept in a thick stand of pine until well into morning. Between him and Packer lay three days' ride, but if the weather, the Comanches and the Cannibal Owl cooperated, he would make it to Goodnight well within Porter Fairchild's deadline for saving old Jay's neck. Sometime during the eighth day appeared likely.

Arriving in Ackerly, a cow town holding down the southeast corner of Dawson County, he stopped to rest, feed his horse and himself and send a telegram. The sad-eyed little clerk behind the counter in the grubby cubbyhole that passed for the local Western Union office read his message.

" 'Have got back property, will get there soon. Signed J.S.' Can I make a suggestion, mister?"

"Do."

"You can save two words by dropping 'have got back' and replacing it with 'recovered.' "

"Good."

"And 'will get there' could be arriving, saving two more."

"Good."

The man sucked the stub of his pencil and sent it flying across the form. "Let's make it 'Property recovered stop arriving soon.' And initialed J.S. That'll be twenty-five cents."

Slocum paid him, requested and was given a pencil and piece of paper, thanked the man and ten minutes later was back on the road. He rode, slept under the stars, spared his horse unnecessary exertion, avoided unnecessary delays, stuck to the road and on the morning of the eighth day had come within roughly five miles by estimate of Goodnight.

Locating a saddle rock split into nearly equal halves and guarded by a lone loblolly pine, he dug a hole under the tree and buried the red envelope, taking care to remove one stock certificate and tucking it inside his shirt. Glancing about, he drew a map, added compass directions and stuck it in his pocket. Filling in the hole, he smoothed the dirt carefully until it blended with the surrounding ground. Ten minutes of rain would wipe the evidence away completely, but whether it rained or not before the Fairchilds got there the chances of anybody else stumbling on it were remote.

He approached Goodnight from a more northerly direction than he departed, feeling it more prudent to avoid the main road so close to town. His route brought him within sight of the local cemetery. Noting the road dividing it, he decided to continue on it into the town situated less than a mile beyond. A funeral was in progress. A small knot of black-clad citizens gathered around an open grave. A plain pine coffin sat on its ropes on the ground alongside. The minister was leading the assembly in a hymn:

Rock of ages, cleft for me.
Let me hide myself in thee.

Lowering his head to make himself as inconspicuous as possible, Slocum started through the cemetery. He began reading the grave markers along either side. Pulling up short, he jumped to the ground and ran up a rise, stopping in front of two newly placed markers. In front of one was piled a fresh mound of dirt. Swallowing hard, feeling the blood quickly draining from his cheeks, his heart thumping wildly, he read the inscription.

RIP
JAY PACKER
BORN 1840
HANGED 1881

"Jesus Christ no!"

Next to it, overlooking an open empty grave, the other marker read:

RIP
JOHN SLOCUM
BORN 1843
HANGED 1881

14

It came as a shock, an emotional convulsion jumping to life in his eyeballs, beating and burning swiftly down his body, on down to the balls of his feet. Sight of Packer's grave shook Slocum. Sight of his own, yawning invitingly beside it, suffused his whole being with the feeling he was crumbling into small fragments.

"The bastards, the bastards, the bastards, the bastards, the bastards," he whispered hoarsely. "They done it, strung up poor old Jay, poor helpless son of a bitch! Flung their own preset time limit into the trash and shut him up permanent!" And they were just waiting for *him* to show up to pull the same business one more time.

The coffin across the way had been lowered, the benediction said, the dust scattered, the diggers beginning to fill in as the mourners dispersed, breaking off into groups of twos and threes. Slocum wearily made his way back down the rise to the road, waving, calling an elderly man away from the group and over to him.

"Morning, mithter," said the man, baring his naked gums. "Whath up?"

Slocum indicated. "Those graves up there. I come all the way from Colorado looking for them two. What's all the hanging about?"

"Bad bithness, let me tell you. Them two robbed the bank, thtole more'n twenty thouthand, every thent moth of uth had in thith world. The law catched one of 'em and wath holdin' him, but when word got out a bunch buthted into the jail, hauled him out and thtrung him up."

"No trial, no nothing?"

"Well they athed him where he'd hid the money and he didn't tell tho—" The man shrugged self-consciously and stared at the tips of his boots.

"His partner got away—"

" 'Pearth tho."

Slocum flashed the deputy's badge he'd picked up in Seminole. "I'm obliged to you. See you around."

The old man touched the brim of his Stetson in acknowledgement and Slocum mounted up, swung about and rode off.

The Fairchilds. Nobody in town but the two of them even knew about the "robbery." One or the other had to have planted the rumor about the missing savings, dropping the blame squarely into Jay Packer's lap. The townspeople must have gone wild. With the result that old Jay was now six feet under and his buddy Slocum had come within a baby's eyelash of joining him and might yet if he didn't make fast tracks.

"The dirty pricks! Probably the two tallest pillars in the whole damned community washing their hands in the blood of an innocent man," he murmured. His hand went to the stock of his Winchester. How he'd love to ride back that night, search out the two of them and gun them down like rattlers in the road!

"I'll get 'em, Jay boy, if it takes the rest o' my days! I'll see them hanging so high the fuckin' buzzards won't be able to get up to 'em! Goddamned sons o' bitches!"

He was shouting now, roaring over the mild thunder of his horse's hooves. His heart hammering, the blood rising to his face, his eyes misting over.

15

Once he got bridle and bit over his temper, Slocum's first impulse was to ride back to the split rock, dig up the envelope and burn every last stock certificate. Meager vengeance, perhaps, but classifiable as a start. But even before he could bring himself to turn the horse in that direction, second thoughts assailed him. Maybe it made more sense to leave the envelope where it was, at least for now. He certainly couldn't convert the certificates into cash, into even a $100 for all $20,000 worth. He'd have to make contact with somebody in some bank somewhere, preferably out of state —some fine upstanding citizen as greedy and fraudulent as Turnbull's brother-in-law—before he could even consider dumping the damned things.

The Fairchilds. To think they'd actually expected him to ride back into their town, envelope in hand, had actually figured him to be that stupid! No, apart from the one under his shirt, he'd leave them lay, in spite of his temporary poverty. The silver dollar keeping company with the crudely drawn map and the deputy's badge filched in Seminole wouldn't take him far, certainly not the 300 miles to Eagle Pass. So he'd have to put 50 or 75 miles between his horse's ass and Goodnight, stop off and find work picking cotton, cutting sorghum, even ranching for eight bucks a month and bunk and board.

Texas! He loved the goddamned state, every foot of it. Yet every time he crossed over into it he ran smack into one kind of hornet's nest or another. Getting his ass picked up for rustling longhorns, for screwing the goddamned mayor's wife in Austin, getting chased by vigilantes mistaking him for somebody who'd turned over a Wells Fargo office. The list of infractions petty and grand, legitimate and erroneously attributed, was long and impressive, and now that he paused to reflect on it made him wonder why he'd ever wandered back in the first place.

"See Texas and say hello to trouble," he muttered.

Into the second hour he slowed down to spare the horse. By late afternoon he managed to cover a good 50 miles and over the remaining hours of daylight made six stops at six ranches asking for work. The lucky bug jumped out of the deck at the last door he knocked on. A gray-haired, gray-faced woman with the look of death in her pink-circled eyes shook her head negatively, then just as she was about to close the door, changed her mind and pulled it wide open.

"You might try the Hanley spread. Jed Hanley lost one of his hands early this week. Poor soul passed away of the pee-neumonia. I understand Jed pays top dollar."

"Thanks, ma'am. Whereabouts would that be now?"

"The Hanley spread. Double-Haitch Ranch. About four mile down the road just outside Wilbo. You can't hardly miss it, son, they's a big double haitch painted on the silo."

"I'm obliged to you, ma'am."

"Good luck. Say, you look hungry."

"I—"

"Care for some fresh apple pie? It's just outta the oven."

Slocum was famished and mention of fresh apple pie triggered the juices in his mouth like spring freshets bursting to life. His throat closed as he swallowed, and the tip of his tongue began negotiating his lower lip.

"Sounds mighty tasty."

"Just set yourself down on the stoop." She brought out a fat slab of steaming hot pie sitting on a flowered plate alongside a shiny clean fork. "If you don't swally every last crumb you'll hurt my feelings now. I cain't stay jawing with you. Got other pies coming out. When you finish, just leave the plate and fork on the stoop."

"Will do and thanks again."

He ate the pie with enormous deliberation, savoring

each piece to the fullest, letting the breeze cool each forkful, then sliding it into his mouth. The slab was fair-sized, but the taste so delicious, so mouth-wateringly delectable, he could have downed six full tins, enough to pop the buckle from his belt. He was down to the last forkful, lifting it from the plate and examining it in the light of the dying sun, when around the corner of the house came six dirt- and sweat-caked hands, their shoulders hunched in exhaustion, faces grim, eyes spiritless.

As one man they stopped and stared, watching him put away the last morsel, withdraw the fork and lay it across the empty plate. If ever he had seen envy and disgust in strange faces, these gawking faces captured both reactions entirely.

A single thought raced behind all twelve eyes: *We been bustin' our nuts since sunup and back we drag to this beggin' bastard sittin' on the stoop, relaxin' hisself, enjoyin' free handouts! A lazy, good-for-nothin' freeloader!*

As the staring continued, Slocum swallowed, wiped his mouth, set the plate and fork down, got up, found the brim of his hat with his index finger, nodded, mounted up and rode.

Yes, Jed Hanley could use a hand. The pay was ten dollars plus board. The work varied. At the moment he and one other hand were busy rebuilding the well. He kept 40-odd head of shorthorns and a wallow full of pigs. He doubled as vet to the owners of the other spreads round about and was forever hopping into his buggy and running off to deliver a calf or foal. Or drop a dose down anything with four legs and a few with two. Like any of the other five hands, Slocum would be expected to drop everything and accompany him when summoned. And, warned Hanley, wind up playing midwife to some overfucked mare or assistant vet to some damned bull afflicted with Bang's disease and as sterile as a petrified egg. Hanley was raising a barn and sowing oats in his north forty. The house fence was in need of repair, postholes had to be dug and stumps blown out of a spread earmarked for corn the next spring. He listed 16 additional daily chores and half again that number requiring sporadic and weekly attention. Breakfast was at five-thirty, lunch at noon on the job—whatever the job—supper at six sharp, and "if you can keep your eyes open after eight-thirty, you're a better man than the others. But seriously, if you ain't lazy, if your back's strong, your mind's weak and you're capable of raising as good a set o' blisters as the next hand, you got yourself employment."

Slocum fought down a sigh and accepted. To think it would take him the entire month to salt away ten lousy dollars—which, well-stretched might be just about enough to get him to Eagle Pass—was a prospect dangerously close to scary. He could have held up the damned Western Union office in any one of 16 towns he'd passed through earlier that week and walked out with 50 times that sum in one hand!

He could have snatched $20 from the safe in Turnbull's brother-in-law's office that night in Seminole, instead of a damned tin badge. Worse yet was the nagging recollection that $20,000 worth of stock certificates was sitting in a certain envelope at the foot of a certain pine tree near a certain split rock. Those certificates were good-as-gold paper that any businessman with the slightest suggestion of larceny in his soul would likely give him a thousand dollars for. If, that is, he was stupid enough to dare approach anybody.

Still, he mustn't lose sight of one important extra benefit offered by accepting this job. The Double "Haitch," as the sickly looking pielady called it, would provide an excellent hideout from the Fairchilds—should they take it into their heads to scour the area around Goodnight for the only man still alive who could finger them as the real culprits for the crime for which poor Jay Packer had been hanged.

"You're making a wise decision," said Hanley, rocking forward in his chair and slapping Slocum on the knee. "Like I say, the work ain't easy and there's no shortage of it, but we got a good group here. No kids, no females. And come the end of the month that ten dollars looks mighty welcome. There's just one other point."

"What?" asked Slocum in a weary tone. The mere explanation of the different jobs, their number and variety, had tired him out.

"That arsenal you're carrying, your .44 and the Winchester. I'd appreciate you handed 'em over to me. I'll lock 'em up for safekeeping for you. You'll have no use for 'em 'round here."

"The Winchester okay, but if it's all right by you I'd prefer to hang on to my pistol. I'd feel naked without it. Besides, it might come in handy out in the fields. You know, snakes and varmints and the like."

Hanley pursed his lips, wrinkled his brow and considered this. "Well, if you really feel you'll have use for it. But I'll thank you to keep it unloaded, with the cartridges in your pocket. Anytime anybody's temper flares up, which is bound to happen once in a while, I'll have no gunplay."

"I'll keep it empty, word o' honor."

"Fair enough. Now then, if you leg it out into the kitchen, you can be first in line for evening grub. When you're done eating, I'll show you around the spread, and you'll probably want to turn in early. The cook'll start banging the old triangle bird early in the morning. You'll have your hands full tomorrow, I promise you!"

16

Hanley's promise was good. But as Slocum was quick to discover, it wasn't the amount of toil, nor even the overly onerous demands of most of the chores on back, limb and wind—hauling posts, digging postholes in hardpan, hand-lugging 200-pound coils of two-point Glidden barbed wire and the like. It was the abject lowliness of certain jobs, such as swamping cigar butts, whiskey vomit and sputum that missed the spittoon out of the bunkhouse—and slopping the hogs first thing after breakfast.

Slocum knew hogs, all breeds, all ages from long experience. Their distinctive repulsiveness, their affinity for mud and garbage, their ravenous appetites and their continual grunting and farting and shitting and pissing placed them, in his opinion, far down the patriarch Noah's ladder of likable creatures, the top rung of which was reserved for the horse. Slopping hogs wasn't difficult. A four-year-old imbecile able to lift a pail and dump it could handle the job. But it was precisely this aspect of it that got him down and kept him there. The job was so goddamned demeaning, so disgustingly vulgar and base. And such a blatantly obvious reminder of how far down he had sunk in recent days. From a man well-heeled from a job well done, owner of a fine horse, a superior saddle, a rifle and pistol bought and paid for with cash, a man endowed with good health, peace of mind and the respect of his fellows, he had come down to hiding out under an assumed name, his assets depleted to a silver dollar and a batch of stolen stock certificates and faced with the prospect of 30 days' slave labor in order to earn enough money to run far enough to escape the hangman.

Where, he wondered ruefully, was justice in this world?

That evening he downed supper and fetched his arnica-covered multitude of aches and pains, pulled muscles, sore back and feet into his bunk, falling asleep with his clothes on.

The next morning arrived, he swore, no more than three hours after lamp-out snoring started. The biggest, the ruggedest, the most painful chore he'd yet encountered fell to him when he tried to lift his tortured body up out of bed. He made it. To breakfast, and after that to slop his friends near their wallow behind the barn. He worked most of the morning with another man, transferring a small mountain of cowshit into a heavy-duty box-brake wagon.

Then after the midday meal he was assigned a patch of land that had to be cleared of cottonwood stumps. The outer roots could be chopped free with an ax, but the taproot was concealed under the bulk of each stump and had to be dug to and blown loose with dynamite. Under the broiling sun, working with his shirt off and sweating like a stuck hog, Slocum quickly decided that wielding the ax was unnecessary labor. Why not let the dynamite do the bullwork, separate all the roots from Texas. With this in mind, he jammed no fewer than three large sticks of Pritchard down the next hole, lit the fuse and stood clear.

The dynamite lifted the stump—well over two feet in diameter—clear. And taking with it what appeared to be most of the field surrounding it. The stump rose like a three-pound cannonball at Shiloh, higher and higher still, coming down some distance away. It missed the barn by a scant margin, but landed squarely in the hog wallow, killing a gilt, maiming a boar and bringing Jed Hanley and his foreman, a big Swede from Minnesota, running out. Slocum stood with his fingers in his ears trying to block out the ringing.

The Swede was prepared to knock Slocum's head free of his neck, but Hanley took the whole thing good-naturedly, patiently cautioning him to detach each stump with a single stick only. And promising not to deduct the cost of the gilt from Slocum's monthly salary.

Slocum continued freeing stumps until after four in the afternoon. Hanley came out for a second visit, this time driving his gig with Slocum's horse tied to the tail-gate. Balancing the ax head flat against his bare shoulder, Slocum approached him.

"Stick the ax and the dynamite sack in the back and

get your shirt on," said Hanley. "I want you to ride into town for me."

Slocum tossed the ax in, fetched the dynamite and his shirt, untied his horse, mounted up and moved forward. Hanley handed him a list of items, his signature penned with a flourish at the bottom.

"What about money?" asked Slocum.

"You won't need any. Just give that list to Tom Chapford at the general store in Wilbo. He'll make out a list just like it with the price across from each purchase. That he'll give to you." Hanley dug a battered satchel out from under his seat. "Put everything in here." He winked. "I'll expect to see you first thing in the morning."

"Much obliged, Mr. Hanley."

"Just make sure you don't get so drunk you forget the satchel someplace. Better shake your stumps, the store closes at six o'clock." Again Hanley winked. "Have a good time, y'hear?"

Slocum thanked him again and rode off toward Wilbo. For all the wrack and ruination of his body and the iron vise of fatigue squeezing it mightily, the prospect of a night on the town was just what his spirits needed. He had stuffed Hanley's list in his breast pocket and riding along with his reins in his teeth, he opened the satchel. It was empty save for a single paper dollar lying at the bottom.

"Mr. Jedediah Double-H Hanley, you are one charitable-hearted human being, sir," he said aloud, perking the horse's ears. "I'm purely grateful to you."

Wilbo turned out to be half the size of Goodnight, a lazy little cow town erected around a saloon, a fairly disreputable-looking hotel—its sign hanging by one hook—a general store, a stable, a sorghum storage depot and the sheriff's office.

Slocum made straight for the store, tying his horse, climbing the steps and venturing into four walls, a ceiling and floor stuffed with goods—racks of clothing, legions of farm tools and equipment, myriad assortments of drygoods, nostrums and household essentials and three aproned clerks serving upward of a dozen customers. Slocum reached the shortest line and eventually the counter, setting the satchel down and handing Hanley's list to the clerk.

"Mr. Chapford?"

"He ain't here." The man glanced at the signature. "It's okay. Doc Hanley's signature is good for all the credit we got to give. Let's have a look at what he wants. One set octagon brass ox balls; six copper bull rings; one Fuller Calf Weaner; one No. 1200 Hill's Pattern Hog Ringer; one pair D 824 Wolf Tooth Forceps; two D 866 jointed Seton Needles; one three-bladed, brass-handle Horse Flems; one D 822 double-edged Hoof Knife; one can Bigelow's Purple Jack; two boxes Gall Cure. . . ."

Slocum's attention drifted away from the clerk to a pert-looking woman standing behind a bust half again too big for her body, but a treat to the eyes to start a man salivating. As if suddenly aware she was being stared at, she swung about showing a butt broad enough to eat Sunday breakfast off of, and bent over a baby carriage, inspecting its interior.

Slocum's mind wandered out of the store and across the street to the hotel with her on his arm, up the stairs and into bed, the pair of 'em stripped raw.

"Mister—Mister, I'm talkin' to you!" snapped the clerk with a tinge of annoyance in his tone.

"Sorry, friend."

"I'm saying we got everything exceptin' the bull rings. Them we're fresh out of."

"Yup."

"Did you hear me?"

"I—" Slocum pulled his eyes away from the well-rounded display and nodded at the clerk. "Sure, yeah. You got everything but the—"

"The bull rings."

"Right."

He waited while the man filled the satchel, watching the curvacious customer wander about examining the merchandise. Then he left the store.

As he stood by the front door surveying the town by the light of the dying sun, he was surprised to see her appear seconds later. She did not even look in his direction as she started across the street, heading for the Wilbo Hotel and Restaurant. Like a well-trained puppy, he tagged along at her heels. Halfway across, his eyes lit on the wanted dodgers cluttering the bulletin board alongside the door to the sheriff's office.

Any man who lived the type of life John Slocum lived found it all but impossible to resist looking over the wanteds in every town he passed through—looking for friends, looking for himself. Such a pastime was almost a reflex. Either you knew without question, and were pleased and proud that the world also knew that nobody wanted *you* for so much as stealing a half-starved yardbird or you suspected or knew absolutely that the contrary was the case.

Slocum knew no such thing as the latter. Today marked the tenth day of Porter Fairchild's time limit. It hadn't held for old Jay to be sure, but it had to hold for John Slocum, considering the fact that $20,000 in stolen stocks hung in the balance. He had until midnight that night to show up. So it was with both shock and amazement that, in approaching the bulletin board, the very first dodger to come into focus announced a $5,000 reward for none other than John Slocum:

WANTED FOR BANK ROBBERY AND MURDER

JOHN SLOCUM

> $5,000 reward for information leading to Slocum's arrest and conviction for the robbery of the Goodnight Farmers and Merchants Bank or information leading to Slocum's arrest and conviction for the murder of Horace Turnbull in Seminole, Gaines County, Texas.

Any person with information regarding Slocum's present whereabouts is advised to contact his local law officer, Sheriff Tyson Fairchild of Goodnight or Sheriff Bob Walz of Seminole directly.

Caution, Slocum is armed and dangerous!

There was a picture of him. Not a very good likeness, but good enough. Somebody had painstakingly described him to the artist. Somebody or his brother.

17

Slocum's first reaction came fairly close to outright panic. Suddenly everybody in the street, everybody in town, was big-eyeing him. A hundred eyes burned into the back of his head. Any second now somebody, probably the sheriff himself, would walk up and grab his shoulder. Tilting the brim of his hat well down over his eyes, Slocum spun about and, head lowered, started back toward the general store.

Putting the pieces together didn't demand any deep thinking. Packer must have let slip to one or the other Fairchild that Turnbull had mentioned a brother-in-law banker in Seminole. And once he, Slocum, got off that telegram telling them he'd recovered the stocks and was on his way back to Goodnight, Tyson had probably wired Sheriff Bob Walz in Seminole, asking after Turnbull. When Tyson was told what had happened, he lost no time pinning the blame on John Slocum. What it came down to was that with Packer and Turnbull disposed of, only one more obstacle had to be removed.

How they figured nailing Slocum would get them their stocks back was a mystery to Slocum. Maybe papering the state with his picture, and the promise of $5,000 to anyone grabbing him, was their idea of insurance. They had to be reasonably sure he'd come riding back into town. Maybe tabbing him for Turnbull's murder was designed to prevent his leaving the state, if, after sending the telegram, Slocum changed his mind about coming back.

But why would he do that? There was no way possible he could have assumed Packer was already dead.

On the other hand, maybe they'd lost interest in the stocks and were willing to sacrifice them in order to remove *him*. Maybe the $22,000 alone satisfied their greed. Maybe—

Jesus Christ, it was all too confusing. How in hell could you figure what was in somebody else's head? The only thing he could be certain of was that he suddenly had a fat price on his head, and once they got him in custody, back in Porter Fairchild's pocket, he could start counting the hours to his lynching.

Strapped for money or not, he had to make tracks, a mess of them, all the way to the Mex border and well over it. Arriving at the counter at the rear of the store, he set Hanley's satchel down on it. The clerk who had waited on him earlier gestured greeting.

"What's up?"

"Would you do me a favor, fella?" asked Slocum. "See that somebody gets this satchel back to Doc Hanley? He's expecting it first thing tomorrow morning. I can't make it back. I got personal business I got to attend to."

"Mr. Kreitsman can deliver it. He rides by the Double-H on his way into work."

"Much obliged."

Slocum headed for the stable. He hated the thought of leaving the area without his Winchester, but going back to the ranch for it would mean he'd have to tell Hanley he was quitting. He'd have to explain a whole long string of ridiculous bullshit. Time would be wasted. No, the quicker he got out the better.

He rode inside the stable, out of sight of the street

traffic, before dismounting. The stableman was a swarthy middle-aged man as lean as a hoe handle, with wild black eyes that darted nervously about. He was sitting on a nail keg, cleaning a horse brush and puffing on a corncob pipe that raised a stink that all but overpowered the stench of horseshit.

"Mexican rice root," he said. "Best damned horse brush money can buy. Better than palmetto. What's on your mind, mister?"

Slocum laid one fond hand on his saddle. "How much?"

The man got up, setting the half-cleaned brush and his pipe on the keg and inspected the saddle.

"Cost me sixty bucks," said Slocum in a hopeful tone. "Practically brand spanking new. Look at that ornamentation, the stamping. Those stirrups are brass-bound."

"Give you ten bucks."

"Jesus Christ, man, it's got to be worth at least thirty! Look at how new!"

"If I got to buy it, it might be worth thirty, but I don't. You got to sell it. Ten bucks, take it or leave it." Recovering his pipe from the keg, he began puffing, eyeing Slocum through the smoke with an annoying leer of triumph.

"Twenty!" snapped Slocum, "I mean I've only had the fucking thing two months. You can see for yourself, it's got every stitch in place. Not a one close to worn. Look at that cantle, solid as stone. You can't bend it back with both hands."

"Ten dollars."

"Fifteen!"

"Twelve."

"Fuck you." Grabbing his reins, Slocum turned the horse and started it out the door. Pausing in the doorway, he let out a long breath, his shoulders drooping, his obstinacy deserting him. "Oh to hell with it, I'll take it. Twelve it is."

"Ten."

"What the fuck! you just said—"

"You just said fuck you. That'll cost you a dollar a word. You don't come into a man's place o' business and insult him. No sir, that you dasn't do. Not me leastwise."

"I'm sorry I said it," said Slocum glumly. "I apologize."

"Ten dollars."

"Jesus Christ, you're a hard man, you know that?"

The stableman smirked, produced a wallet and counted out ten greenbacks. "How 'bout the blanket?"

"What about it?" asked Slocum.

"Comes with it, don't it?"

"In a dead pig's ass!"

18

To hell with towns, reflected Slocum, as he rode away bareback. And to hell with Mexico, at least for now. He was a hot new face up among the wanted dodgers, and $5,000 was a healthy inducement to drop hoe, hammer or hayfork and start looking. For that amount it wouldn't surprise him if half the population of Texas was already lining up along the border from El Paso to Brownsville waiting for him to show.

It made a good deal more sense to head back into the Comanchería and cross over into New Mexico. Night riding it all the way. Come morning he'd be 70 or 80 miles from Wilbo. He could locate a cave or a dense stand of trees and sleep away the day. He could buy food for himself and the horse at the back doors of farmhouses. He'd need never venture near anything like a settlement. Every damned town had some kind of law officer and a board of wanted posters and public-spirited citizens with eyes in their heads.

Over the red land he rode, the mesquite, sweet-smelling creosote and oak bushes witness to his flight. The staring stars and moon emerged from a sky as black as the pit. He passed through an area resplendent with the subtle beauties and mysteries of nature: tortuously twisted trees with flaming red bark, others with orange bark, delicately drooping junipers, giant yuccas and music among the murmuring breezes disguised as the call of the kingbird and the cooing of the white-fronted dove. But in his preoccupation with his dilemma his mind was closed to all sounds and sights save the road ahead.

Riding and eating by night, sleeping in a cave concealed in a stand of loblolly pine, he made his way to within 50 miles of the border, on the opposite side of which lay Hobbs, a town he knew well. It was an all but lawless town where wanted dodgers were disposed of moments after they arrived on the stage.

He awoke the afternoon of the third day, his spirit buoyed by having evaded capture so far. He pinned the deputy badge on his pocket, ran a hand over his week-old beard, grateful that it changed his appearance, and headed west, riding some 200 yards parallel from the main road. Rounding a sandstone out-cropping lacerated by wind and weather and crowned with three stunted oaks, he came upon a man straddling the right foreleg of a handsome big-beamed bay. He stood, examining its hoof, letting it drop at Slocum's approach, and looking up.

It was no man but a lovely woman, an eye-stopping beauty with a complexion like cream, sparkling green eyes and golden hair tucked up under her Tower Stetson.

"He seems to have picked up a stone."

Slocum pulled up and dismounted. "Let's have a look."

It was a pebble the size of the tip of his little finger. It had lodged between the buttress and the shoe. Using the tongue of his belt buckle, he pried it loose easily.

"It may be sore for a day or so, but it's nothing serious," he said, letting the hoof drop. "You can ride him okay." She stood watching him. Straightening up, he turned to her, smiling.

His face froze. In her hand was a chrome-plated .38 pointed straight at his heart.

19

Her hand flashed out and snatched his .44 from its holster.

"Well you're welcome, I'm sure," said Slocum.

"I'm turning you in, mister." She smiled, showing beautiful teeth and a full-lipped mouth ideally made for loving, all sorts, all parts. At the moment, though, she didn't appear to be in anything like an affectionate mood. She explained that she was a bounty hunter.

"A she-male bounty hunter?"

"That's what I said."

"That's crazy!"

"Don't fool yourself, Mr. Slocum. I make a tidy sum tracking down wanteds." Reaching inside her saddlebag she brought out a familiar-looking flyer. "John Slocum, double count, robbery and murder."

"Who's John Slocum?"

She grinned. "Who indeed?"

"I never heard of him. Let me have a look-see." He took a step forward, bringing up one hand. She waved the .38.

"Keep your distance, friend." She tossed him the dodger. Bending, he picked it up and studied it, pretending puzzlement.

"You think I'm this guy? Lady, you're confused. I mean all mixed up in your head. Take a good look."

"Let's stop playing poker, Mr. Slocum. I picked up your trail the other side of Wilbo. You made a bad mistake sleeping away these past three days. You should have been riding night and day. I'd have been, with five thousand dollars on my head."

"Who the hell are you?"

"Mind your language. I can't abide a foulmouth. The name is Letitia Pray, Letty to my friends."

"Whoever heard of a bounty hunter with friends?"

"Hands behind your back."

"Aw, come on—"

She waved the gun. "Mr. Slocum, let's get one thing straight right off. I'm holding the gun. That puts me in charge. When I tell you to do something, you do it. If you don't do it the easy way, you'll do it the hard. Either you put your hands behind your back this instant, or I smack you over the head, put you to sleep and put them behind your back for you. Understand?"

"Yeah."

She tied him expertly, one-handed, with a two-foot length of rawhide.

"That's too damned tight! You're cutting off the blood!"

"Don't fret. If your thumbs fall off, I'll loosen it. Mount up."

"Where we going?"

"To the nearest town. I make it Lassiter Junction, about fifty miles north."

They rode for 20 minutes, the yellow sun filling itself with orange and starting down behind the Davis Mountains to the west.

"I'm hungry as hell," said Slocum. "Can't we stop and cook up something hot? I'm purely dying for a cup o' coffee. I got half a tin in my saddlebag. You're welcome to share."

"Why not?"

They stopped near a lazy, pathetically small stream. Letty loosened his bonds, cautioning him against any "foolishness," and suggesting he gather firewood while she prepared supper for the two of them. He wandered a circle around the two horses, loaded his arms with sticks, stacked them over a pile of dried millet grass and lit it.

She had apples and fresh biscuits to go with his coffee. The crowning touches were a red and white checkered tablecloth, freshly ironed, napkins with the initials L.P., clean silverware, salt and pepper shakers and china plates with painted gold edges and bluebirds in the center.

"This is better than the Palace Hotel in St. Louis," said Slocum admiringly. "It's sure gonna make them rocks taste better. What do you say to laying over the night here? I mean, by the time we get to Lassiter Junction it'll be closed up tight. Why wake the sheriff up out of a sound sleep when you can turn me in just as easy tomorrow morning?"

"You're full of advice today, aren't you? You wouldn't be playing for time, would you?"

"What the hell good is time with my hands tied behind my back? All the same, turning me in tomorrow bright and early makes good sense, don't it?"

"Doesn't."

"What the hell's the difference?"

"Foulmouth!"

"Apologize. Lady, if you think hell is swearing, you don't know what foulmouth is."

"I had a father and four brothers."

"If you don't mind my asking, how'd you ever get into bounty-hunting? Why?"

"Every man I pick up is curious about that. Every blessed one. If you must know it was because I hate housework, cooking, sewing, laundering. I like horses, riding, my .38—"

He cut her short with a snide laugh. "I'll wager you can't hit a barn with that handful o' tin."

Drawing the .38, she leveled it at a cluster of prickly pear cactus standing some two hundred feet away, and through the gathering gloom picked off a yellow flower with one shot.

"That's good shooting."

"That's a lot of practice, Mr. Slocum. I can shoot with any man, ride with him—"

"I reckon you can kick and scratch and scream with the best."

"There's no need for that if you know how to handle a gun, is there?"

"Good point."

"At the risk of sounding proud, I consider myself as good a shot as the best man I've ever come up against. This year alone I've already brought in eleven wanteds. And without picking up a scratch. In fact the worse thing that's happened to me or Twinkle—"

"Who?"

"My horse."

"Twinkle?"

"Twinkle. Is that pebble he picked up back where I caught up with you."

"Where *I* caught up with *you*."

"Not at all. I circled around and got in front of you earlier today."

"You stick that stone in your horse's shoe to trick me into stopping and dismounting?"

"No, that was just a fortuitous happenstance."

"A which?"

She stifled a yawn and excused herself. "I seem to be a trifle sleepy."

"You got to be tired. Women don't naturally have what they call a rugged manly constitution."

"I can go without sleep for three nights running. I have."

"Still, don't it make sense to bed down here for the night and take me into Lassiter Junction tomorrow morning? Besides, there's such a thing as the condemned man's last wish."

"I wouldn't be so flippant about it if I were you. You happen to be in a great deal of trouble. We'll stay over here if you wish, but you realize I'm going to have to tie you hand and foot."

"Of course."

They finished eating, she washed up and they talked. She told Slocum that she had originally come from Montana, up around Helena. She had wandered down the territories looking for work as, of all things, a ranch hand, but had been laughed off one spread after another without even being given a chance.

"Every man's job I asked for—farming, mining, even deputy sheriff—I was turned down cold. And ridiculed and insulted by some of the sorriest misfits in Christendom. Only because I happen to be a woman."

"A very beautiful woman."

"Mmmm." She was too vexed to be impressed by compliments.

"The trouble is, I mean what you don't seem to understand is that a woman's place is in the home."

Bristling, she glared. "Who says?"

"Everybody."

"Well 'everybody' is misinformed!" She jabbed her chest squarely between her breasts with her thumb. "This woman's place is precisely where she wants it to be!"

"You're buckin' the tide."

"Eleven turnovers in less than eight months. Bank accounts in seven cities. You call that bucking the tide?"

"Well you got to admit you got the element of surprise working for you. You're the last one in the neighborhood a wanted man would suspect would be after his ass. Oops, foulmouth, I know. Sorry."

"Don't imagine I don't use my appearance to advantage. Every chance I get."

"You a man-hater?"

"So would you be, so would anyone."

"You didn't answer the question."

"No!"

"Ever have a boyfriend?"

"Certainly, dozens. There's business *and* pleasure. I'm normal, if that's what you're getting at."

"You're a beautiful woman."

"I believe you already said that."

"I mean it."

"Thank you." This was said flatly, in a matter-of-fact and slightly bored tone. A long pause followed. A whippoorwill's call drifted down the night, and the stream burbled quietly, contentedly as it eased by.

"Can I ask you something personal?"

"Hasn't that been the general tenor of your inquiries thus far? What now?"

"You ever wear a silk dress? You know, something to show off your figger?"

"Not in some time," she said wistfully. "I pack only what I need."

"You should wear a silk dress, maybe red and black with flowers all over it. You'd look a real lady."

"You think superficial assets like clothes make a lady?"

"You know what I mean."

"Mmmm." Again she covered a yawn and excused herself. "I'm afraid that's all the talk for tonight. I'm going to have to turn in now."

At her direction he lay on his right side, his hands above his head. She tied his wrists around a slender cottonwood. Then she secured his ankles.

"How come my ankles? I ain't about to walk no place with this tree."

"Anyplace."

She squatted on her well-rounded haunches, staring down at him, the moonlight filtering through her long blonde hair—released from imprisonment under her Stetson—the breeze nudging it gently.

"You're all man, Mr. Slocum."

"Every part, Miss Pray."

"Letty."

"John."

"Why did you do it, the murder, the robbery?"

"I didn't do either one," he explained.

"I'm not surprised."

"You don't believe a word."

"Actually I do. You don't appear to be, you don't behave like the violent sort."

"I'm no wing-backed angel, but I'm sure innocent o' this nonsense. Though I'll have a hard time proving it."

"Maybe not so hard. If there was a way to find out what that banker and his brother are up to, what they're doing with the money. What you'd eventually have to get is a written confession."

"Easy said, but not so easy done."

Suddenly, wholly unexpectedly, she leaned over and kissed him on the mouth, the warmth of her lips pressing his firmly, her tongue driving into his mouth and thrashing about. Then slowly she freed her mouth, murmuring contentedly.

She kissed him again and a third time, each time longer than before, more ardently.

"You have a nice mouth, John."

Slipping her hand down to his crotch, she undid the buttons, pushed inside and began fondling his balls, stroking them, caressing his cock. It began stiffening. Abruptly she got up, went to her saddlebag and took some things out. In the darkness he couldn't see what. Going to the stream she came back to him seconds later with a small basin half full of water, a cake of pink soap and a small towel. Without a word, without so much as a glance his way, she unbuckled his belt, pulled down his denims and, setting the basin within reach, began lathering his cock and balls. The fragrance of the soap resembled apple blossoms, but so captivated was he by the ritual and so enjoyable was the sensation of cool soapy water laving his privates, he resisted commenting. Completing her ablutions, she tossed out the soapy water and rinsed him clean with clear water. Then, drying him thoroughly and leaving him hanging out balls and all, she restored the basin and soap to her saddlebag and came back with a small bottle of what appeared to be perfume.

It was. "*Nuit*," she said, holding it up for his approval. "*Parisien*, fifteen dollars an ounce."

Shaking the bottle, then removing the top, she daubed his cock and balls with the fragrance. Then placing the bottle to one side, she arranged the towel neatly under his balls and kneeling down, took the head of his cock into her mouth.

She was fabulous. He had never been eaten so slowly, with such deliberate and calculated gradualness in all his years. Abusing it magnificently, she got his cock as hard as a button-head king-bolt and throbbing fit to burst its head, and make Slocum lose his mind. But, lying propped up on one elbow, watching with fascination, Slocum decided that no words he could utter, no persuasion, no power on earth could induce her to speed up.

Nor did he want her to. She took a full 30 seconds to ride up from the base of his cock. Slowly releasing his head, she turned to sucking his balls, encompassing one then the other with the ring of her lips and gently punishing each in turn with her tongue.

Presently she began biting, nibbling away at the most tender portions and areas of scrotum, of cock length, of head, restoring it to the hot wet socket of her magnificent mouth and resuming the slow steady pace of sucking. Down in the depths of his balls his come began whipping to a boil, building his jewels to the hardness of steel. He came, projecting his load up and out, pulsing and sloshing furiously against the back of her throat and down it. And seconds later he was limp, her mouth deserting him, her hand replacing it, gently stroking balls and cock, working to bring them back to life.

"Easy," he whispered in the voice of exhaustion. "Them three old boys has been through a lot."

"The night is young, John. That was just the appetizer. Only the beginning."

20

Over the course of the next full hour, she ate him practically continuously, with hardly a pause for breath. He lay, feet and hands tied, panting audibly, enjoying every moment, every electric movement of her mouth and lips and swollen tongue. Her appetite for his come appeared insatiable. Again and again she gobbled him, all but ingesting his cock and balls completely. At length, finishing him off, she raised her head, tossed her hair, freeing her face of it, and smiled bewitchingly.

"There. That's for you."

"Letty—"

"Now for me. I want to feel you inside me, John."

"Feel what, tapioca pudding? Lady, I got nothing left in me but dead air. I couldn't come dust!"

"Then I'll just have to help."

With that she began caressing the limp length of his cock, fondling his balls, slowly refilling them. Then she resumed teasing his cock with the tip of her tongue, building stiffness into it.

"I can't do nothing for you all trussed up like a calf. You're gonna have to untie me."

"That won't be necessary. You just lie on your back, I'll mount you."

"It still won't work. I got to be able to spread my legs."

She hesitated. "Very well, I'll free you. But don't imagine you're going to get away. You'll have to exhaust me completely, so that I drop off to sleep." As if this observation served to remind her of how tired she was, she yawned again. And excused herself in ladylike fashion.

Slocum ran it through his mind. Once down in Cerralvo he'd seen a Mex bitch take on 42 hardrock miners one after the other as quick as they could get it off. Then get up on her feet, down a pint of tequila and dance without stopping for the next three hours. Sad to say in his experience there wasn't a man living who could fuck any cunt, two-legged or four, into exhaustion. As unfair as this may have been, it was nature's way.

But by her own admission, she had been riding

night and day pursuing him. She couldn't stop yawning. She'd even come right out and admitted how tired she was before she began eating him. He, on the other hand, had slept practically the entire day, and apart from the fatigue investing his jewels, he was well rested.

She untied him and the two of them stripped naked. Mounting her, he drove it slowly home into her dripping cunt. He'd do it, he resolved, if he could just keep it up, hard enough to stave off thrust buckling. He'd do it. He'd pound her until she passed out. Then button up and ride out.

She was most eager to cooperate, grinding and gyrating like a mongrel bitch on fire. Pushing, shoving, driving against him, engorging his cock. The instant his cock had found its way into her vagina she took over, orchestrating the act, dominating Slocum, losing all control, scratching, biting, her beautiful eyes enormous, as wild looking as a starved cougar's, every part of her in violent motion, her great breasts jiggling mightily, a patina of sweat setting them glistening under the pale light of the moon.

They fucked and fucked and fucked. Each time Slocum swore to his maker, to heaven and hell that there was no possible way he could get it up "just once more," but he did. Or rather she did it for him. For reluctantly reflecting on it in the midst of it, he sheepishly confessed to himself that from the very first thrust it became all her. From the onset it was all he could do just to hang on. He let her have her way with him, as if the swollen, throbbing, overworked and scandalously abused member connecting them wasn't his to begin with. It was hers, sprouting from her cunt and fucking his balls, cudgeling them to a bloody pulp, pounding them to raw bits!

Most disheartening was the obvious fact that she looked to be getting stronger as he weakened. From some hidden reservoir within she brought up fresh reserves of energy, dismissing her earlier fatigue.

Forty-two hardrock miners, one after the other as quick as they could get it off. A pint of tequila, three hours dancing—

21

The sun slammed against his sealed eyelids, triggering pain suggesting two needles thrust cleanly into his eyeballs. His hand fumbled its way up his chest, reaching his eyes, shading them. He rose on one elbow yawning, glancing about. He was naked, his clothes strewn around him, the dead fire at his feet, his horse grazing contentedly on buffalo grass beyond.

There was no sign of her bay, no sign of her. Nothing even to suggest that she had been there, save for the wanted dodger. Torn into four pieces it lay beside him. There was a penciled note scrawled on the back of one of the pieces. Four words:

"Thank you. Good luck."

Gratitude blending with relief swelled within him, but immediately became somewhat diluted when he couldn't spot his gun. Or his cartridge belt. It didn't make sense. Why would she let him go and leave him unarmed? Maybe in leaving, dressing, packing up, saddling up she'd simply overlooked the .44. But whether it was absentmindedness or a conscious play calculated to remind him of who had been in command all the way, it came down to the same thing: it left him defenseless.

He washed, dressed, made coffee, let the horse drink from the stream and got back on the road to Hobbs. He figured he would be reaching the border in a couple hours, leaving this lovable hellhole Texas in his dust. The border. It represented no real protection, actually; it was only a geographical division between state and territory. Texas had to stop somewhere. It couldn't butt up against California, Minnesota, Florida. So whoever owned the pencil had decided to limit its westward advance to a line running south to north, closely paralleling, for the most part, latitude 104 degrees.

There would be wanted dodgers featuring his handsome likeness in New Mexico. But fewer of them and fewer law officers willing to give up their round-backed chairs to run him down in this heat—although Porter Fairchild's $5,000 reward was generous bait. Riding through creosote and mesquite, the sun burning into his left shoulder, he reconsidered, then altered his plan. Despite its reputation for lawlessness, Hobbs was too big for his liking, too chancey. Slocum would've preferred some cluster of shacks widening the road, containing a handful of citizens working so hard keeping body and soul together, the kids fed, the pigs slopped, the cow milked, that nobody had time to worry about wanteds. Slocum recalled towns like Humble City, no damned bigger than a gopher hole and a lot less active.

Bypassing Seminole, he followed the Mustang Draw to the New Mexico line and crossed over. He had covered a couple hundred yards, and was still reveling in the thought that he was no longer in Texas, when he came upon a strange sight and a stranger-looking old man in command of it.

DR. TALLYBOROUGH'S HOMEOPATHIC MEDICINE SHOW
WORLD'S FOREMOST ENTERTAINMENT
FAVORITE OF PRESIDENTS
AND THE CROWNED HEADS OF EUROPE!

Sprawled across the once-white bonnet of a wretched looking Conestoga, in faded, painted letters a foot tall, the message jumped from the sun-drenched landscape like a wildcat from a ledge. Slocum reined up to read it again and permit his eyes to take in the sight of the man. He was leaning against the rear wheel of the wagon, resplendent in a well-wrinkled round-cut sack suit, patent-leather shoes with opera toes, a stovepipe hat rising a good 14 inches from his brow and foot-long snow-white hair draping down over his shoulders. He was holding a banjo, strumming away and singing in a well-cracked baritone:

> She took me in her parlor,
> she cooled me with her fan;
> She whispered soft in her mother's ear,
> "I love this gambling man."
> "Oh daughter, oh dear daughter,
> why do you treat me so?
> To leave your dear old mother
> and with a gambler go!"

Lowering his banjo, he tipped his hat, revealing a crop of hair to rival the snow atop Pike's Peak.

"Behold, a knight errant of the open road, a perigrinating pistoleer of the Plains astride his *equus caballus*. I bid you good morning, sir knight."

"Howdy."

Walking to the rear of the wagon, he placed the banjo inside and gestured Slocum closer.

"Come, dismount, join me in a cup of Crushed Java Coffee. It's my very own blend, brewed for me by a Javanese gentleman of my acquaintance, a most flavorful beverage."

In all his years, Slocum had never heard the English language so eloquently spoken as Dr. Horatio Woodley Tallyborough spoke it. Every single-syllable word magically became three and four syllables, every two-syllable word five and six. The man's mastery of the mother tongue was extraordinary, his ability as a banjoist less impressive, and his knowledge of his present whereabouts nil.

"We're still in Texas, are we not?"

"No, sir. Didn't you see the marker up the way?" Slocum indicated. "Up yonder behind that creosote bush." He sipped his coffee, savoring the delicious flavor, vowing on the spot never to drink his own coffee again as long as he lived.

"Missed it completely. My optometrist in St. Louis has advised me to invest in a stronger spectacle lens.

Biolateral myopic astigmatism, you know. A common affliction in one of my advanced years."

Dr. Tallyborough let it be known that he was down on his luck. A succession of minor catastrophes had caught up with and overcome him. One of his mules was ill with a touch of pox.

"A rare malady amongst mules, but not unknown."

Infinitely worse was the fact that Madame Zora, his gypsy fortune-teller who tripled as Scheherazade, belly *danseuse* and Mademoiselle Erna, Snake Charmer Extraordinary, had run off with the Masked Marvel, also billed as Mister Mystery, the doctor's heavyweight boxer who at every performance took on all local challengers and generally disposed of them in one round.

"If the yokel manages to remain upright for a full two rounds, he is rewarded with twenty-five dollars."

"Anybody ever do it?"

The doctor winked and grinned, showing more gold than a lucky forty-niner's pie tin. Reaching inside his coat he brought out a small brown bottle with a red cork. Slocum studied the label.

"DR. H. W. TALLYBOROUGH'S
SYSTEM BUILDER
&
LUNG RESTORER
GREATEST VEGETABLE TONIC
OF THE AGE
AVAILABLE ONLY FROM DR. T.
BEWARE OF SUBSTITUTES!"

"What in hell is it?" queried Slocum.

"Mostly colored water with two or three of nature's stimulants. I insist that each and every challenger fortify himself with a healthy swallow before entering the ring."

"You mean you build 'em up? You make 'em stronger?"

The doctor shook his head, smiling roguishly. "Not

this bottle. It's loaded with chloroform. It was Max's idea."

"Max?"

"Max Lichtenberg, the Masked Marvel. The motherless miscreant has left me in the lurch, the two of them. How sharper than a serpent's tooth—" He was in the process of restoring the bottle to his pocket when he stopped short, staring at Slocum. "Say, you wouldn't be interested in gainful employment, would you?"

"You got to be a mind reader. Right at the moment I'm practically tapped out."

"How fortunate for the two of us. Ahem, today is Saturday. By five o'clock I hope to reach Hobbs, where I'll be setting up shop, dispensing my nostrums, fortifiers and medicines off the tailgate. Alas, the Greatest Entertainment in the West promises to be something less than entertaining, now that my cast has deserted me. I shall get right to the point, young man. I'll pay you five dollars cash for every yokel who challenges you in the ring."

"Me take on all comers?"

"Precisely."

"No thanks. Christ Almighty, I could get what few brains I got scrambled like hens' eggs in ten goddamned minutes. I could get outright killed!"

"Not a chance." Out came the bottle a second time. "One swig each and they'll all knock themselves out. All you're required to do is tip them over."

"Maybe so, but I'd still be sticking my neck out."

"How? I don't understand."

"We're too close to Texas. I'll level with you. I got a fat price on my head over there. For me to stand up in the middle of a Saturday night crowd showing this face to everybody would be asking for trouble, begging it!"

"Ah, but you're wrong. The Masked Marvel never shows his face. He wears a hood with slits cut for the eyes. It's all part of the window dressing. A touch of mystery, intrigue."

"Nobody'll see my face?"

"Not a living soul."

"And I won't get my head knocked off?"

"Not unless an anvil falls on you."

"Did you say five dollars?"

"At least a hundred on a Saturday night. It's all psychological, you see. Every time you kayo one yokel, the next one fancies he's discovered a flaw in your defense and can't wait to climb into the ring. And you know these farm boys. They start early, become thoroughly inebriated by eight o'clock, feel obliged to display their pugilistic prowess to their friends, particularly their lady friends. They step right up, down the proverbial hatch, into the ring and—"

"Whammo!"

"I assure you, they'll collapse like tenpins. They always do. It'll be the easiest money and the fastest you'll ever earn. Are you with me?"

"It's a deal."

"Excellent." Dr. Tallyborough rubbed his hands together gleefully. "Ladies and gentlemen, proud citizens of this great and thriving metropolis—"

22

"It is with pride and pleasure that I introduce to you the one, the only, the original Masked Marvel, the pugilistic Man of Mystery, Champion of six continents, superhuman Wonder of the Western World!"

Slocum stood on the tailgate stripped to the waist. He threw his chest out as far as his pectoral muscles would allow, and raised his fists which displayed iron bracelets encircling his wrists. Around his waist was a thick belt holding up his flaming red skin-tight drawers. He was sweating buckets under the woolen hood, staring out at the mass of upturned faces, wide eyes and open mouths. Alongside the wagon a ring had been erected. Dr. Tallyborough continued declaiming in strident tones:

"The Masked Marvel is prepared to take on all comers, the biggest, the strongest, the most courageous Hobbs has to offer. One at a time, needless to say. Step into the ring. The bell will sound and challenger and champion will come out fighting. Should the challenger prevail for two complete rounds, a total of four minutes by this time clock I am holding in my right hand, the battle will be declared over and you, you or you"—his upraised index finger impaled three onlookers in quick succession—"will be awarded the sum of twenty-five American dollars!"

Five crisp five-dollar bills appeared in the doctor's right hand.

"You need not render the Masked Marvel *hors de combat*. That, alas, has never been done—not once in the one-thousand eight-hundred and forty-two fights preceding the first engagement here tonight. The challenger need only remain upright. Should he be knocked down or fall down, the bell will ring and the fight will be declared over. And one more victory will be added to the remarkable skein of triumphs compiled by the one and only Masked Marvel!

"Now then, who among you considers himself man enough to step forward and challenge the Masked Marvel?"

"He don't look so danged tough to me!"

"Ahah, challenger number one. Will you step forward, sir?"

A bloat-bellied farmer in bib overalls, his shoulders as wide as the horns on a longhorn and hands, when laid side by side, big enough to cover the same creature's rump, detached himself from the crowd.

"Your name, sir?"

"Oswald Pettingill Junior."

"Oswald Pettingill Junior. Ladies and gentlemen, let's have a rousing round of applause for Oswald!"

The crowd responded with applause, huzzahs, catcalls and crudities. Somebody in the rear punctuated this outpouring of sentiment with an outright insult.

"Hit him with your beer belly, fat boy. You'll knock him into Eddy County!"

Oswald did not take this good-naturedly. Turning away from Dr. Tallyborough he started through the crowd, fists high, an angry look on his moon face. The doctor grabbed his sleeve and with surprising strength pulled him back.

"Hold everything. The twenty-five-dollar fight is up here."

Slocum groaned. The fat son of a bitch looked capable of turning over a stagecoach full of bricks with one punch. He wouldn't be able to move worth a goddamn, but getting past that balloon gut to reach his jaw appeared to be no cinch. If he couldn't get over it maybe he could get around it. A good lick to the side of his jug head, fill it full of stars, and goodbye, Oswald.

"But before the fisticuffian festivities get under way, with your kind permission, ladies and gentlemen, permit me to introduce another reigning champion, a *nostrum par excellence*, the liquid of life, the ambrosia of Ajax. Famed far and wide for its amazing properties and powers, the one, the only, the original Dr. Horatio Woodley Tallyborough's System Builder and Lung Restorer!

"Yes, good people. Here in my hand is the wonder tonic of the age, a secret blend of nature's most remarkable remedies. With a hundred applications, each more marvelous than the last.

"For the cure of coughs, of chronic and lingering bronchitis, laryngitis, consumption, ulcerated throat, sore throat, hoarseness and suppression or loss of voice. It neither nauseates nor debilitates the stomach or system, but invigorates and cleanses the system entirely. As a remedy for torpor of the liver and for habitual constipation of the bowels it has no equal. As an alternative or blood purifier, this formula is far superior to sarsaparilla, iodide of potassium or any other medicine presently offered for general sale.

"Above all this marvelous tonic instills great strength and instantaneous power into the system of any and all who imbibe but a few drops. King Luis of Portugal and the Emir of Arabia both endorse its miraculous curative, restorative and strength-building properties. I have here a letter from Her Majesty, Queen Victoria of England, congratulating me and expressing appreciation for sending six bottles to Prince Albert during his recent illness. As all of you are aware, I'm sure, the prince is now hale and hearty again." He held up the letter. "Her majesty credits his recovery and, ahem, newfound potency in the royal bedchamber, to the contents of this little bottle in my hand. One dollar, ladies and gentlemen, greenback or silver, will obtain for you a six-months' supply of this marvelous System Builder and Lung Restorer."

Six full cases emptied rapidly, a blizzard of greenbacks descending upon the doctor. Oswald Pettingill Junior was prevailed upon to down a dose in preparation for the fight of the century. He did so, stepped into the ring, swung once, swung twice, slipped, fell like a well-aimed battering ram flush against Slocum's fist and went down so hard he all but sprung the four corner posts from their moorings.

Five dollars for this, mused Slocum happily, was like stealing. Five more challengers followed Oswald to destruction. Not one managed to last into the second round. Why nobody in the crowd seemed able to connect each challenger's hasty collapse to Dr. Tallyborough's dosage surprised Slocum. But nobody did. And on the mere three hours' sleep that Slocum had managed to sneak after arriving in town, he felt strong enough to wallop the world.

If a woman can take on 42 hardrock miners and drink and dance for an encore, why shouldn't a man be able to knock down 42 stumblebum citizens? Especially with the assistance of the little brown bottle with the red cork? Nature was all checks and balances, wasn't it? Of course.

Number seven stepped forward: a grinning, handsome kid no more than 17, about 200 pounds, medium height but as wide as Oswald and with upper arms bigger around than most men's necks. With him was a pretty red-haired girl who obviously idolized him and was petrified at the idea of his stepping into the ring.

She pleaded with him and tugged at his arm. But the kid was not to be dissuaded. It was his chance to be a hero. Wild mustangs couldn't hold him back. And a mere taste of the System Builder was not enough. To Dr. Tallyborough's chagrin, the kid seized the bottle from him and promptly emptied it down his throat. The doctor flashed a worried look at Slocum, eyes announcing the possibility that drinking so much so fast might possibly render the boy permanently unconscious.

He stepped over the ropes and lifted his fists in the time-honored pose of Jim Figg and his legion of successors. The bell rang and the fight started.

But it was no fight. It was carnage, slaughter. The kid's right caught Slocum full in the face, smashing his nose and splattering the area surrounding it with blood, blinding John. His left found Slocum's throat, all but closing it against the top of his spine. Suddenly he couldn't swallow, couldn't breathe, his head swam, his brain careened about inside his skull. Great flashes of red and orange, purple and yellow shot out in all directions.

And still the kid came at him, pounding him mercilessly, egged on by the screaming crowd. Slocum couldn't see, couldn't breathe, could barely hear. The only thing he could do was feel—pain, excruciating pain rooting in his nose and flowering inside his skull, exploding in his larynx and fixing a steel band around his neck, quickly tightening, threatening to close so snugly it would sever his head from his body.

He went down, hard, like a two-ton tombstone. The back of his head hit the canvas, driving additional pain down through his brain to his shattered throat.

And out he went.

23

"I'm at a loss for words." Dr. Tallyborough had been groping, so far without success, for something stronger than a mere apology. "Nothing like this ever happened before."

Slocum groaned.

"I was very careful. I gave him a newly opened bottle. He drank every drop. I stood staring at him—"

Groan.

"And after he—knocked you out and I'd given him his money, he walked off with his young lady on his arm without so much as a drop of perspiration on his brow. And not the slightest ill effect. A physiological phenomenon if ever I've seen one!"

Groan.

"Not so much as a yawn. As bright-eyed as if he'd just gotten out of bed. Remarkable! If I hadn't seen it with my own eyes—"

Groan.

"Total immunity to chloroform."

Slocum lay flat on his back in the bottom of the wagon, surrounded by the paraphernalia of the business and neatly stacked empty "System Builder and Lung Restorer" cases. His head propped up on two pillows, a horse blanket draped over him, he was a helluva sight. His throat black and blue from the base of his chin to his breastbone, a rectangular court plaster draped over the fragmented remains of his nose and stuck to his swollen cheeks. The doctor had painstakingly washed away the blood, set the nose, cleared passage in both nostrils, permitting the patient to breathe and otherwise rendered Slocum as comfortable as possible.

He remained, however, in pain.

"You're a lucky man, John."

Slocum wondered if the doctor had suddenly taken leave of his senses.

"I'm serious. By some miracle, your esophagus was not shattered. You can talk. Try."

"Mmmmmn."

"Syllables, words, go ahead. I know it's sore."

"It—feels—like—barbed wire being pulled up and down, scraping the sides."

"Give it a little time."

"Every rib busted."

"Only four and not badly. I taped them up."

"My nose?"

"It's broken. Very very broken. While you were unconscious I did my best to restore it to something resembling the original shape. I did a very artistic job, if I do say so myself."

"Feels rotten."

"It will, for another week or so. Be patient, let it heal. The important thing is to protect it. Leave the plaster on and stay out of bars and other public gathering places. I shudder to think what might happen if you got into a fight."

Slocum lifted himself up on his elbows and stared at the doctor. His words continued coming out with noticeable strain.

"What am I supposed to do, wear my hat on my face?"

"Don't take it to heart. You'll heal. I'm just saying be extra careful. Treat yourself as an ambulatory patient. Baby yourself."

"I never hit him, not once. When he hit me I thought a damned boulder wall was falling on me, burying me!"

"Forget it. Cheer up. You're thirty-five dollars richer. Look on the bright side! With those two black eyes, those swollen cheeks, the condition of your throat and that bandage across your nose, your own mother wouldn't be able to match you with the picture on the wanted poster." The doctor counted out $35, folded it once and, pulling the blanket down, stuffed it into Slocum's shirt pocket. "Now then, what are your plans?"

"I plan to lie here for the next three or four months."

Tallyborough laughed. "Give yourself a few days; get plenty of rest. You'll come around. I'm moving on to Bernard." He waved one hand about the interior. "We did a tremendous business here, nearly seventeen cases. I'm going to have to get out the vat and whip up a fresh batch of System Builder. There's an idea. Maybe you should have a dose."

Slocum didn't hear. He'd dropped back to sleep.

He stayed with Dr. Tallyborough long enough to permit his body to pull itself back together and his bruises to fade. The doctor treated him royally, ministering to his every need and taking conscientious care of his horse as well. When Slocum finally felt up to riding again, he insisted on reimbursing Tallyborough for the expense the doctor had gone to on his behalf, pressing $20 on him. The wagon stood at a crossroads on the border of Chaves County within sight of the Mescalero Ridge, the oppressive noonday sun dumping its fire down on both men.

"Keep it, John. You don't owe me a cent. You'll need it."

"Fifteen bucks'll do me fine," said Slocum, stuffing the rest into the older man's hand and curling his fingers over it. "I still got a few bucks left outta the ten I left Wilbo with. Hell, I'm loaded." Slocum leaned down from his horse and shook hands. "Good luck, doc. Hope you find yourself another Masked Marvel, somebody who can handle himself a little better than the last one."

"I wish you'd keep that court plaster on your nose for another few days."

"It itches like hell."

"Try and stay out of trouble." Tallyborough tilted his elongated stovepipe hat one way then the other. "Your beard is getting positively bushy. That's an excellent disguise."

"Don't fool yourself. Every guy on the run sprouts a beard. Any smart lawman can spot a suspicious character through six pounds o' hair."

"Wear your badge. Tell everybody you're out looking for John Slocum. Seriously, are you heading down to Humble City as you planned?"

"I reckon. It's the only town around these parts they still sell five-cent whiskey."

"Good luck, John. It's been a pleasure knowing you."

"Been nice knowing you, doc. Not painless, maybe, but nice."

24

Rounding a bend in the dusty road, Slocum came within sight of Humble City, sprawling alongside the railroad tracks, a water tower in full view. A single red-feathered arrow was stuck into the base of its tank at a jaunty angle, proof that other Indians were not the marksmen the Comanches were. The railroad tracks reminded Slocum of the single certificate neatly folded inside his shirt against his healed but still slightly sore ribs.

Then his thoughts flew ahead of him to the Silver Dollar Bar in the center of town with its cut-rate bar whiskey that set a man's teeth on edge as it slithered past but was hot honey going down. One other feature of the Silver Dollar jumped to mind, the flaming-haired nude reclining above the bar mirror—in Slocum's opinion, the most voluptuous-looking woman in all the territories. If she actually existed, if she hadn't sprung full-grown, fully developed, barren of attire from the artist's mind, if she was living, breathing flesh and blood, wandering about the West, he'd have to bump into her sooner of later. He lived in the hope. He'd been doing so for 15 years.

But a jarring disappointment was in store for him as he tied his horse and made his way through the batwing doors into the Silver Dollar. The lady still reclined, still smiled, not a hair turned, not a dimple out of place. But to Slocum's annoyance her breastworks and her lovely lower regions were now concealed under two adroitly draped gold silk cloths.

Bellying up to the bar and ordering his whiskey, he learned to his irritation that the price had doubled. Rattling a dime to rest, he downed half his drink. Getting the bartender's attention he asked him why the lady in the frame was under wraps.

"I become a Baptist, brother, dunked and full-fledged. Us Baptists don't permit wanton exhibition of the female torso."

"Why don't you just take her down?"

"No reason to do that. Don't you think she's got a right purty face and a well-turned ankle?"

"There's other parts more interesting." Slocum glared. "If you went and become a Baptist, what about strong drink?"

"Not a blessed drop, brother."

Slocum swept the bar with one arm. "What the hell you call this, tea time?"

"Don't abide cussin', neither. As to strong drink you'll notice it's all being swallyed on *your* side. Nothing on mine, not since six weeks ago tomorry."

Slocum produced a dollar bill. "Gimme a double."

"Bless you."

Considering the earliness of the hour, the saloon was crowded. A piano jangled raucously against the end wall and three card games were in full and spirited swing. The crowd was lively and happy. Occasionally a drunk would slump to the floor, be raised, righted and delivered to a chair or assisted out the door. The man standing elbow to elbow with Slocum suddenly pushed against him, sloshing the remainder of John's drink over his hand and attracting the bartender's rag. Turning and scowling at Slocum, the culprit pushed a meaty forefinger against his chest.

"Why don't you watch what you're doing?"

"Me? You was the one shoved. Spilled half my drink, you clumsy asshole."

"Who you callin' an asshole?"

"The one I'm looking at with the rotten teeth in it. Want to make something out of it?"

No sooner had he said it than a sharp twinge of regret overtook him. He remembered too late that his nose wasn't quite up to punishment of the sort that can be administered by short stroking at close range. It still ached furiously when he sneezed.

Luckily the drinkers crowding the bar were so tightly compressed, neither Slocum nor the shover was able to back away far enough to bring up their arms and swing freely. So Slocum decided.

Unfortunately the other man neglected to accept this, obvious though it was. Forcibly elbowing room for himself, he raised two fists that resembled small anvils with knuckles. The man drove the left one into Slocum's shoulder, and he was dispatching the right straight for his jaw when John jerked out of the line of fire just in time, the fist whirring by his ear. He got his hands up to protect his face when to his surprise the gold head of a cane came driving down, slamming his attacker full in the pate, dropping him where he stood.

"John Slow-Come!"

Slocum gaped. Standing before him attired in an expensive steel-gray suit and vest, interlined celluloid collar and cuffs, shiny new Russian calf shoes with toes sharp enough to open envelopes, and a neatly brushed, curlbrim derby hat was a friend Slocum hadn't seen in ten years.

"Rip Ripley. Well I'll be dogged!"

Stepping over the pile of unconscious man, Slocum grabbed, the newcomer grabbed, and belting each other's arms fondly both began roaring laughter.

"If you ain't a sight to see!" exclaimed John. "All decked out like a Frisco pimp!"

Thorne Ripley. His mind hurtled back over the years to the first time they'd met. In a bar in El Paso. Confronting each other as total strangers, they had locked horns within minutes, becoming embroiled in a bruising and bloody toe-to-toe set-to over a busty little brunette. The fight had wound up in a draw, the two of them all but collapsing from exhaustion, coming around with a stiff shot of Taos Lightning to discover that the prize for which they'd been battling had walked out the door with a notions drummer from New Orleans. Conversation led to an all-night drinking bout, to skull-splitting hangovers that rendered breathing pure torture. There followed a full year's close association up and down the territories. That was terminated when Ripley was picked up by the marshal in Denver for a stage holdup he hadn't been within 40 miles of.

They settled down in a private room over a bottle of imported Scotland whisky.

"How did you ever get outta Canyon City Penitentiary?" asked Slocum.

"Simple, they found the fella who really did the job," said Ripley, distorting his unnaturally homely features into an expansive grin. "We looked enough alike to be brothers."

"The poor bastard!"

"How would you like a punch in the nose?"

"No thanks. You stood a whole year. How come you couldn't come up with an alibi?"

Ripley downed two fingers of Scotch, licking the residue from his mustache. "The judge gave me three years for that job. My alibi woulda gotten me five. At the time they figured me for the stage holdup, I was holding up the Wheat Ridge Express Office."

"Oh my. But look at the old boy now, them duds, that gold-headed cane."

"Raised ornamented Polo Crook, all the rage in Europe. Imported from London. Blink the booze outta your eyes, Mr. Slow-Come, you're lookin' at Humble City's most successful business tycoon."

"You a business tycoon. That'll be the day."

"Laugh if you like, but that's the deal o' the cards. I happen to be exclusive territorial representative for the Winchester Repeating Firearms Company, home office New Haven, Connecticut. I control the lion's share of the oil rights in Lea, Eddy and Chaves counties. I own forty percent of this saloon. I'm on the verge of becoming a member of the board of directors of the Southern Pacific–Texas and Pacific Railroad."

"You're what!" Slocum slammed both hands down so hard the bottle danced and fell over, Rip catching it neatly without a drop spilling.

"Easy, Slow-Come."

Slocum brought out the stock certificate, unfolding it, spreading it wide and turning it around so his friend could read it.

"Southern Pacific–Texas and Pacific Railroad. Any good?"

Taking out a pair of pinch glasses, black ribbon and all, Ripley focused through them. "Looks legal as all hell to me."

"You better bet!"

He told his story, pouring out every detail in chronological order, re-experiencing the hell and the happiness of it verbally. Ripley cut in early.

"Jay Packer dead? Lynched?"

"That's what happened, though you can't blame the depositors. It was Fairchild's doing. It had to be."

"I can't believe it." Ripley's normally rosy complexion paled visibly. "It's just not possible. Some fellas you meet you figure for indestructible, you know what I mean? So tough, so wily, so fast moving the old man with the scythe'll never be able to catch up with 'em. Old Jay was one."

"He didn't get caught up with, Rip. He got bushwhacked for fair. That heartless son of a bitch tossed him to the wolves."

"Tell me the rest of it."

The telling took them to the end of the first bottle and halfway through a second. Ripley sat in stunned silence, his shaggy head shaking slowly, his cow eyes expressionless.

"Whatta mess o' snakes. Jumping Jesus!" He ticked the high points off on his fingertips. "Knocked out and robbed by a whore, tricked into busting open a safe, double-crossed by your friend, going after him you run into Comanches, talk yourself outta gettin' skinned alive, find the fella, shoot him, get the stocks back, go back and find Jay dead and your own grave open alongside his waiting for you."

"He framed us for stealing the twenty-two thousand dollars *and* the certificates."

"Going on the run, hiring out for slave labor, winding up with a robbery and murder price on your head, getting picked up by a female bounty hunter—which has to be true on account it's too wild for a feeble brain like yours to cook up—gettin' fair fucked bowlegged. You lose your rifle, your pistol, your cartridges, your gunbelt, get screwed outta your saddle, get the shit kicked outta you by some hay pitcher and wind up nearly gettin' your head busted up a second time."

"If it hadn't been for you."

"You'd be wearin' your nose on your ears, I know. Slow-Come, you been an active man. I mean all over the landscape! Jumping Jesus, fella, can't you do anything right? Doesn't anything good ever happen to you?"

"I'm just running a string o' bad luck, that's all. Happens to the best."

"Bad luck? Jumping Jesus, you're writing a whole new book on it! You've found yourself enough for half a dozen guys. Now you're in up to your ears. How you plan to get outta it?"

"I been so busy running I ain't had much time to think about it." Slocum drained his glass. "This Scotland whisky tastes mighty good, you know that? Smooth as a tit."

"Forget the goddamned Scotch. Let's get down to cases. One thing you done right: you managed to get outta Texas. Now what?" Slocum shrugged, staring at Ripley with a look in his eyes that was more an appeal for help than puzzlement as to the correct answer. "You got one ace up your cuff."

"I'm outta Texas, sure."

"No, no, no. Jumping Jesus, did that farm boy in Hobbs bust your brain as well as your nose? This." He tapped the stock certificate lying between them. "Ever think about contacting the rightful owner?" Pausing, Ripley glanced at the signature. "Seth Weatherly. You know him?"

"Hell no."

"You know of him? I mean does he live around Goodnight?"

"He must, I mean, to have his stock kept for him in Fairchild's safe."

"Listen, he could be living in San Francisco or Timbuktu. Your friend Fairchild might just be a close drinking buddy o' his, somebody he trusts like a brother."

"He's makin' a big mistake."

"You know that, but does Seth Weatherly? Evidently no."

"So what do you expect me to do?"

"That's a good question, Slow-Come."

"Will you kindly stop callin' me that?"

"It's your name, ain't it?"

"Push it closer together it is, not Slow-Come."

"I like it. It's got what you call a pleasant ring to it. Slow-Come."

"Oh, fuck you!"

"All kiddin' aside, I think you oughta get in touch with this Weatherly. Tell him what they done to you, give him back his stocks and ask him to help you. If he's got a grain o' decency in him, he'll do what he can to get you cleared."

"And what if he ain't, decent I mean? What if I fork

over his stocks, tell him what's what and he thanks me and slams the door in my face? You figure that's worth taking a chance o' riding clear back to Goodnight for? With the Fairchilds and their depositors and that hole in the ground just waitin' for me to show my handsome face?"

"So disguise yourself."

"As what, the hind end of a stage-show jackass?"

"You got the brains for it."

"Very fuckin' funny! Goddammit, this is serious. We're talkin' about my hide! Five grand on my head. Christ Almighty, I know fellas been shot and boxed for a fraction o' that. So do you." Ripley ignored him, engrossed as he was in examining Slocum's face, crinkling his brow thoughtfully, turning ideas over in his mind.

"I got it! We'll sit you down and shave off every damned hair—head, mustache, that scummy-looking beard, all of it."

"What in hell kinda disguise is that?"

"You'll look different. That's the idea, isn't it? Okay, okay, I'll think o' something else."

"I don't know as I go for this, Rip."

"You got to return the stocks, elsewise you'll be running for the next twenty years."

"If I could get the robbery rap off my neck, shooting Turnbull wouldn't hurt none. It was self-defense."

"You busted into his room, you said."

"He shot first. Okay, we both did."

"Cross that bridge later. Nobody saw you shoot him."

"Nope."

"Okay, I'm takin' over. You just shut your mouth and do like you're told. We're goin' across the street to the Humble House to my suite. I'll be putting you up there anyway. I'll get ahold of a couple friends o' mine to give me a hand."

"Doin' what?"

"Disguisin' you. Slow-Come, you're gonna' look downright beautiful when we get done with you! Grab the bottle and your stock. Move your ass! Jumping Jesus, you could use a bath for starters, you know that? You smell like you been wallowin' with the damned hogs!"

25

By Slocum's standards, Thorne Ripley's suite in the Humble House was the territorial equivalent of a sultan's palace. The only things lacking were eunuchs and veiled slave girls. A large ornately ornamented sideboard, displaying a mirror that John reckoned at 200 pounds, supported a platoon of bottles and fine crystal glassware. A sofa, rocker, armchair and two parlor chairs, generously overstuffed, featured Turkish tassels and gaily colored fringe. Framed landscapes depicting the four seasons adorned the walls, which were papered in gold and maroon vertical stripes. The master bedroom displayed a four-person fourposter bed with a mustang-hair mattress, silk counterpane and no less than six silk-slipped feather pillows lined up against the engraved mahogany headboard. Axminster and Moquette rugs covered the floors. Every room had its own movable chandelier. Sundry expensive-looking tables and smaller pieces crowded the entire suite.

Escorted by his host, Slocum gasped and gaped at this opulent display of creature comforts. Immediately upon entering both men's attention was drawn to the private bathroom off the master bedroom from which came the unmistakable sound of a rat scratching. It was no rodent, however, but a stately blonde in a flowered silk dressing gown standing in front of a mirror scraping away at her teeth.

"Hold it one second, Florabelle," said Ripley. "I'd like you to meet a very good old friend of mine. John Slow-Come, meet Miss Florabelle Sachsenhauser."

"Pleasure to know you, ma'am," said Slocum, baring

his head. He stared at the implement in her hand. Ripley took it from her and held it up.

"You never seen one o' these before?"

"Can't say I have."

"It's a toothbrush," said Florabelle in an amused tone. "For the teeth. Imported from Japan." She displayed her teeth proudly. "I use it with Godsnell's Tooth Cream. It makes my teeth shine pearly."

"You could use one o' these things," Ripley said, shaking the brush. "It staves off rotting."

Miss Florabelle Sachsenhauser took a generous swig of mouthwash, drove it back and forth between her rosy cheeks and spewed it into the washbowl. Then she offered her mouth to Ripley, who removed his long green cigar and kissed her loudly.

"You could use one, Rippy," commented Florabelle.

The hall door opened and another girl came in, not as tall as Florabelle, but similarly well-proportioned, her hair tinted a shade darker than Florabelle's, piled high above her pretty face.

"This is Dorabelle Sachsenhauser," said Ripley to Slocum. "Dorabelle, meet Mr. John Slow-Come."

"Slow-Come? My, that's a pretty name," said Dorabelle, leering and winking.

"The name's Slocum," snapped John, glaring at Ripley.

"I like Slow-Come better," said Dorabelle, crinkling her nose and grinning.

"Me, too, honey," said Florabelle.

"Ladies, Mr. Slow-Come is going to be our guest for a spell. Him and me got a lot o' catching up to do. Dorabelle, you go downstairs and get Leonard to fetch up the plunge tub, some bath towels and a fresh cake o' yellow soap, a big one. And a clean floor brush. You two are gonna give our friend here a bath."

"The hell they are. I can wash myself."

"Not like they can. And after you're presentable we're gonna go to work on you." Ripley ran one hand down Slocum's bearded cheek. "We're gonna dye his beard, his hair, every hair on his body. Red."

"Bullshit!" burst Slocum. "Where the hell did you get that dumb notion?"

"It ain't dumb, Slow, it's smart. It'll be the perfect disguise."

"Mister, I got no liking to walk down the street looking like I was on fire!"

"Old Jay Packer didn't mind it."

"Jay's Jay, I ain't!"

Ripley stared at him. "My mind's made up. We're gonna dye you red if we got to tie you down to do it!"

26

It wasn't necessary to tie Slocum down. He persisted in his objections after his bath, but less strenuously and not at all when Dorabelle stood in front of him, leaning over and swabbing dye into his beard, her breasts jiggling provocatively every time her arms moved up and down. Slocum's mouth went dry as he watched them bounce and bang and bob merrily up and down, the big brown nipples peeking up over the edge of her décolletage every so often.

Ripley and Florabelle meanwhile had drifted into the bedroom, closing and bolting the door. The sound of bedsprings squeaking, healthy grunting and a satisfied squeal could be heard every so often.

"Can I ask you a personal question?" inquired Dorabelle in a serious tone.

"Ask away," said Slocum, his eyes glued to the activity in front of him.

"Do you come slow, Mr. Slow-Come?"

He could feel the color rising in his bearded cheeks. "Is this gonna take long?"

"Almost done."

"Damned stuff stings."

"Don't be a baby. There's a few spots where it's

dripped on your skin. They're gonna have to be scrubbed off. My, you sure do look different. Want to see?"

She took a small beveled mirror down from the wall and held it in front of him.

"Holy Christ, I look weird!"

"No you don't. I think it's sorta attractive. You'll get used to it. Okay, stand up and drop your drawers."

"Huh?"

"I got to dye downstairs."

"No thanks."

"Rip said to."

"I don't care what he said. I don't fancy that stuff dripping on my jewels. That's tender territory."

"Suit yourself. Just don't take your pants off in front of the law."

Using a cotton swab she completed the job, skillfully dyeing his eyelashes. "You'll need another treatment in a week or so. The black roots'll start to show."

"I'll worry about that when the time comes."

She packed the half-used bottle of dye back in its box along with what was left of the cotton. Then, using alcohol, she gently scrubbed away every trace of red drippings on his cheeks, neck, ears and along his hair-line.

"Rip, Florabelle!" she called. "Come and see."

"In—a—couple—minutes!" bellowed Rip from the other side of the door in a voice taut with strain.

Both Ripley and Florabelle agreed that Dorabelle had done an expert job. Slocum, however, was less than enthusiastic over the change in his appearance.

"So I look different, so what? It's still no damned guarantee Weatherly's gonna help me outta the hole. He may go runnin' straight to Fairchild!"

"What for?" asked Ripley. "Fairchild's trying to screw the man. What do you expect Weatherly to do, complain to him? All you got to do is tell him what happened, show him his stocks to prove it, and it'll be all the convincing he'll need. Another thing, maybe part o' that twenty-two thousand dollars cash was Weatherly's, too. Listen, if you're afraid to try—"

"I ain't afraid, dammit. I just don't see any guarantee it's gonna help me none."

"Of course there's no guarantee. But you got to start turning the thing around somewhere. Those stocks are your only card. Tell you what. I got business to clear up, little stuff that shouldn't take more than three or four days. You ride out, see Weatherly, get the ball rolling. I'll follow and meet you, say in Prayerville. Let's make it a week from today."

"I purely appreciate the offer, Rip. But I got myself into this mess, I'm the one should be getting me out."

"And I'm the one should be helping. Jay was my friend too, you know. I always did have a warm cockle in my heart for that sawed-off, loud-mouthed bastard. One week from when you leave, on the hour. Okay?"

"Okay."

27

The dealer sent the cards winging out dexterously, tabling the remainder of the deck and locking it with a silver dollar. The game was two-legged stud, a big pot-builder, since a player had to take two rounds in succession before he could claim the pot.

Six players were involved: four strangers—"riding throughs," Ripley called them—Ripley and Slocum. The game had been organized by Ripley with one purpose in mind. Since Slocum adamantly refused to accept the loan of a couple hundred dollars to finance his crusade, Ripley had suggested a friendly round of poker—unusually friendly toward Slocum, since his friend had seen fit to introduce readers.

Ripley favored edge-work—the cards displaying white margins on the backs, the line separating the margin and the back design being slightly thickened at critical points. A thickening high up indicated an ace, a little lower a king and so on down. From where he sat, Slocum could easily read everybody's hole card. This edge-work edge imbued him with a feeling of power he had never experienced before. It was as if he could see into people's minds and know what they were thinking.

From the very first deal, however, he took special pains to play cautiously, dropping quickly when one or another player paired up on the second or third go-round. The idea was to establish a conservative poker personality in the eyes of the others.

The game was three hours old and he had managed to take four double pots. But rich ones—$102 most recently. He also deliberately dropped a couple. Ripley played with admirable cuteness. Also able to read hole cards, he nevertheless neither won nor lost. One of the strangers, a rawboned, sweat-stained and odoriferous cattle kicker who stopped by on his way through to Albuquerque had dropped close to $400. He was not a gracious loser. He pounded the table, chewed one cigar after another into sodden wads, cursed the cards and came back for more again and again. Slocum might have felt sorry for the man, had he not carried on so.

It was Ripley's deal. He let fly, six cards down, an ace to the man on his left, a six to the big loser, another to the man alongside him, a jack to Slocum, a five to the next man and himself a king.

Pairing his king on the first up card and following with the trey of hearts, Ripley dropped in favor of the loser and Slocum. The loser, Virgil Grantham by name, showed the four and five of spades to go with his down six; Slocum nursed jacks and the nine of hearts. Ripley delivered the fourth card, giving Grantham the seven of spades and pairing Slocum's nine.

Suddenly edge-marking was proving interesting, mused Slocum. Reading the thickened edge position, one could only deduce the value of a back up-card, not the suit. If Grantham's hole six turned out to be the six of spades, he had a straight flush building, if the six of any other suit, a small straight only. This situation was particularly interesting to Slocum inasmuch as it was he who had won the previous hand.

The last card came around, Grantham getting the three of spades, his dark eyes betraying nothing. The jack of diamonds came to Slocum for a full house. Eyeing the pot, he estimated it at close to a hundred, even before the final bets were made. Taking it would give him close to $275, more than enough for his needs. The bet was to Grantham. As Slocum expected, he checked. The sandbag was out and ready. Slocum bet five dollars and caught it in the head.

"Make it twenty-five!" barked Grantham.

"I thought this was a friendly game," remarked Ripley.

"This is a money game; I'm out a wad and friendly's got nothin' to do with it," snapped Grantham. He stared at Slocum stonily. "What'll it be, Red, you calling or dropping?"

"I'm thinkin'."

"Well hurry it up, I ain't got all day."

"I say if one of 'em's got it, the other has to," interjected one of the other players.

"Sssssh." Ripley placed a finger to his lips.

"C'mon, Red," said Grantham testily, "do something."

Slocum's bones announced a bluff. It was the kind of intuitive feeling that comes naturally to anyone who'd played as much high-stakes poker as Slocum had since he was 14. Number one, Grantham was down a bundle. A man in such straits frequently panics and tries to jump back to even instead of carefully working his way to it. Number two, he had already proven to Slocum's satisfaction that he was little more than cornmeal mush between the ears, and had probably persuaded himself that he, Slocum, couldn't possibly have filled up. Number three, Grantham was no stranger to a bluff. He'd already taken one pot in such a manner and a successful bluffer rarely hesitates to try again.

"I call," said Slocum evenly.

Out came the six of diamonds. "Straight."

"Jacks full."

"You motherless fuck!"

Slocum raked in the pot and Ripley the cards, hastily squaring the deck and passing it on to the man on his left. Grantham bitched and bewailed his "rotten luck," scoffed at and slandered Slocum's "blind luck." The new dealer had shuffled, Ripley had cut and the deal was about to start when Grantham lurched to his feet and snatched the deck from the dealer.

"Lemme see them cards!"

"What the hell's the matter with you!" exclaimed the dealer, reaching for the cards, Grantham pulling them farther away.

"Sit down and cool off," said Ripley to Grantham.

Grantham ignored him. He began examining the backs of the cards.

"These fuckin' things are marked. They got to be!"

Ripley stood up, glaring menacingly at him. "I'm the one put 'em in, fella. Brand new, wrapped, sealed and stamped, if you remember."

"Then you're doin' the fuckin' cheatin'!"

"Hey, for Christ's sakes," said one of the others. "Let's stop the shit before we start."

Grantham continued thumbing through the cards, examining them. Gradually his shoulders began to sag and his hands slowed down. Then he sat down heavily, the dealer snatching the deck back.

"Satisfied?"

"Shit."

28

Slocum ran a hand down a latigoe strap, and a finger up the skirt stitching.

"A real bargain at thirty-eight-fifty. Or you can have it with leather over the stirrups for half a buck more," said the clerk eagerly, rubbing his hands together.

"He'll take the leather over," said Ripley. "Nothin' but the best."

As they stood surrounded by saddles in a corner of the store chewing on expensive cigars, Slocum flexed his toes within the comfortable confines of his shiny new high-heel calfskin boots. He also donned a brand new set of clothes: fresh denims, red-plaid shirt and white ten-gallon with brown beading circling the base of the crown. The clerk ran off to fetch the saddle.

"I need these new drawers," said Slocum with pretended weariness. "I like to shit my old ones full when he grabbed the deck. How in hell did you pull the switch? I didn't see nothin'."

"That's 'cause you weren't lookin'," said Ripley, winking. "It was easy as fartin'. You two was jawin' at each other, the other guys were watching you. Hell, I could have switched decks five times. I sat with my balls restin' on the second deck all along, knowing damned well sooner or later somebody would start smellin' the rat."

"I played real careful," said Slocum. "I didn't make it stink. I mean I'd win a few, throw a few, and stay outta most."

"You did fine. Me too. But you know poker; every so often it gets head to head, a real battle. Then it becomes hairy, the loser takes it hard, loses his temper, starts reaching for alibis. First thing you know he's faultin' the deck. You can see it coming. How much did you win?"

"Two-sixty-eight. You?"

"I lost four bucks."

Slocum laughed.

"What's funny?"

"You play poker for three hours with your own marked deck and wind up losing four bucks!"

"It makes sense. We couldn't both of us win, you asshole! Now what else we got to buy you?"

"I been thinkin', I hate to swap my horse. He's a top-notch animal, but somebody around Goodnight might recognize him. Then all this red fur goes for nothing."

"So deal him off. You can always trade back when this business is cleared up and you're off the hook."

"Yeah. And besides the horse, I'll need arms."

The clerk came back with the saddle, ripped the price tag off and handed it to Slocum.

"Light as a feather. See?"

Slocum also bought a Mex combination .44 cartridge and money belt, russet leather and neatly embossed, a matching holster, a brand new Colt Army Double Action .44 and a Winchester, a duplicate of the one he'd left behind at the Double-H ranch.

Ripley protested the last purchase: "I can get you one free, one o' my samples."

"I appreciate it, but I'd rather pay my own way, thanks. Shit, I ain't been this far ahead o' the game since I got rolled by that whore in Wade City."

He also loaded up with ammunition for both pieces. He paid the clerk for the whole shebang, winding up with $201 to add to the $15 he'd arrived in Humble City with.

"All this shopping is making me thirsty," he said to Ripley. The two now stood outside the store taking in the busy street.

"We'll go up to the suite," said Ripley. "Us and the Sachsenhauser sisters can work up a great old drunk together." He winked. "And while you're at it you can get your ashes hauled." He paused. "What are you looking so strange for?"

"Just thinkin'. I wish now I'd hung onto my old duds.

I could keep 'em for a change. You know, wash 'em up real good."

"Horseshit! They was so far gone they couldn't even be burnt. They'd likely start up some kinda poison gas. If you really got to know, I told the clerk to bury 'em."

"You're an insultin' son of a bitch, you know that?"

"Sure."

They started for the Humble House.

"When you figure on pullin' out?" asked Ripley.

"Soon as I switch horses. Sunup, I reckon."

"Okay, we'll get drunk, fuck a little, eat a little dinner, go out and get you a new mount, have ourselves a night of it and off you go."

29

The sun had climbed free of the White River, beyond the Great Plains to the east, when Slocum started out for the Texas border and Goodnight 300 miles beyond. He would dig up the stock certificates, then set out to find Seth Weatherly—rancher, drummer, politician, gambler, whatever, whoever he was. A solid-citizen sort, most likely. Stock and bond holders generally were. And probably located somewhere around Goodnight, hopefully within a 30 or 40 mile radius.

Inquiring from door to door, however, was no way to go about it. And brazenly riding into Goodnight, red-haired disguise or no, would be much too risky. Better he head for the land office at the county seat, corral the clerk with a cock-and-bull story about he and Weatherly being old army buddies, get a peek at the records on the chance that Mr. W. was a landowner and pin down the location.

Presuming Weatherly would be grateful for the return of his stocks, how would that help the returner? How would it influence the law to take down the 6000 "wanted" dodgers, with his old face adorning them and clear him of Fairchild's frame—and Turnbull's killing?

To that he was certain Tyson had linked him purely on speculation. In a court of law, Slocum need not be obliged to prove his innocence; Tyson and Porter and anybody else would have to prove him guilty. And with no witnesses to the deed, getting a guilty verdict would be impossible. He'd tell it to the judge the way he'd told it to Sheriff Bob Walz. Walz and his deputy would corroborate his story. Turnbull's brother-in-law could neither help nor hurt him—being in the dark as he was to all the hairy details. So that was that.

"Shrug it off, Red. Concentrate on the business at hand, getting the goods on old Porter."

How? Good question. Rip might come up with something helpful in the way of advice. He was brighter than anybody else Slocum had hobnobbed with up and down the country. Switching those decks when he did was sure smart. Maybe by the time they got together in Prayerville, Rip will have hatched an idea under that funny-looking derby hat of his.

In spite of his redness, his new outfit, the big stallion he had gotten in exchange for the quarterhorse-plus-$30, Slocum continued to experience apprehension every time he passed through a town and spotted his face tacked to the sheriff's office in company with stage and train robbers, fast-traveling gundown specialists, escaped convicts and other wanted law flouters. He counted no fewer than 13 dodgers between Humble City and Wilbo. Three days later, having come within a mile of the spot where he'd hidden Weatherly's stocks, the total had risen to 20.

Checking his crudely drawn map, he rode up to the split rock guarded by the lone loblolly pine. Dismounting and looking around he marveled at the idiocy of his choice of a hiding place. Anybody riding a mile away in any direction could clearly see his horse, and no doubt him. Closer they'd be able to see him digging, an action certain to arouse any man's curiosity.

His heart began hammering. He'd been in such a grand rush to bury the envelope he hadn't even bothered to check out the landscape. What if somebody had been watching him, concealed behind the mass of mesquite 400 yards to the north or the ridge of sandstone in the opposite direction?

Down on his knees, locating the spot, he began pulling away at the dirt with both hands, opening a hole. He found nothing. He widened it to the left, then up front. His heart jumped as a small red triangle revealed itself. Uncovering the entire envelope, he tucked it under one arm and rode off at a gallop, holding the envelope with one elbow and examining the contents with his free hand.

All safe. Cheered, he mentally crossed his fingers and turned the horse northeastward in the direction of the county seat, putting Goodnight, the Fairchild brothers, the cemetery, poor dead Jay Packer and the empty grave with the name Slocum on the marker, behind him on the right.

He was to discover subsequently that on his way to the county seat he had ridden within sight of and by the Weatherly ranch. By the time he had returned to the area the sun had gone down and he was somewhat hesitant to ride up and present his story to a total stranger. But then he decided that waiting until the next morning couldn't change anything. He might as well get it over with.

It was a fair-sized spread: the house large, painted white with what appeared to be a new roof, Texas yellow roses encumbering trellises on both sides of the veranda and a picket fence surrounding the place. Close by were two barns, a silo, a shed on the verge of collapse, such condition oddly out of place among the other buildings, and a corral, totally empty, the gate standing wide open. There was someone in one of the barns working over a horse, cleaning up. A man and a woman were sitting in rocking chairs on the veranda.

The man was old, grizzled-looking, hunchbacked and slow to rise. Slocum pictured him as a real hellraiser in his younger years, a steady eye, good gun hands, but worn out by hard living, working, drinking, funning, the whole scoreboard.

The woman was half his age: small-busted, well-shaped, not beautiful, somewhere between pretty and plain. Her skin was lovely, but she was tired-looking, as if she'd been up many nights. And there was a cheerlessness about her.

Slocum introduced himself as—pulling it out of his new hat—Roy Finley.

"Is Mr. Weatherly in?"

The woman and the old man exchanged glances.

"My husband passed away earlier this week."

"I'm sorry. My sympathies, ma'am."

"Thank you." She stared past him, her eyes wistful, the corners of her mouth turned down. "The funeral was the day before yesterday."

Oh boy, he thought, this tosses a rat in the stew. Dealing with the man's widow, what would that get him?

"Seth had been ill some time." She shrugged, studying her hands folded upside down against her apron.

He held out the envelope. "These belong to you, ma'am." His eyes wandered to the man.

"Maybe you two'd like to talk private, Alice," said the old-timer. "I got to see about the horses, anyhow. Excuse me."

"Come in, Mr. Finley."

Synonymous with her sadness, the screen door yielded a soft pathetic groan. The house smelled of beef stew, a marvelous odor that never failed to actuate Slocum's taste buds. The parlor was typical, the woman's touch in evidence—the curtains, chair coverings, the large oval rag rug. She offered him a chair by the fireplace, sitting opposite. As she began opening the envelope, a thought flashed across his mind.

Maybe he was going about it all wrong. What did he know about her? Nothing. She could be close as skin with Porter Fairchild. Whether she was or not, what if she refused to buy his story? What could she do even if she did believe him? Her husband would have been a different matter. Fairchild was attempting to cheat him, and—as Rip had suggested—likely stealing money from him along with the stocks. With him he could join forces.

"Is something wrong?" she asked, breaking into his thoughts.

"Er—no." Thrusting one hand into the envelope, she took out the stocks, spreading them in a fan. "They're your husband's. Yours now."

"Southern Pacific–Texas and Pacific Railroad."

"Yes, ma'am. Good as gold they tell me."

"I knew Seth had bought them some time back. Two years ago, as I recall. I've never seen them. He told me—" She stared, a puzzled look.

"How they come into my hands is a long story. If you're interested."

"Tell me."

He did so, leaving the appropriate gaps—Turnbull's death, Letty Pray, other irrelevant points. Stressing Jay Packer's role and his fate. When he was done, she made no immediate comment. Instead she sat immobile in her rocker, staring at the floor, as if she were occupied with absorbing the last of it, taking it all in and considering it. Out of politeness? Slocum asked himself. Interest? Concern?

"It appears you've been pretty badly used, Mr. Slocum."

"Finley."

"John Slocum, dyed hair, beard. I've never seen you before, of course, but it's all over the county that one of the thieves was lynched and the other two got away. The third man was killed, so they say."

"Yes, they're accusing me."

"Did you do it?"

"No."

"You resemble your picture: your eyes, the shape of your face. I gather you think I ought to be amazed by all this." She laughed thinly, without any attempt at humor. "Knowing Porter Fairchild, I can hardly be. I've never liked the man. His eyes, I guess it's his eyes. And his manner. He always reminds me of the villain in one of those stage melodramas, you know, nattily dressed, well spoken, intelligent, attractive, but totally amoral. And so easy to hiss."

"Do you know his brother?"

"Not as well as Porter. He's been out here a couple times on complaints, Tyson I mean. What's truly bizarre is that if you came to me and told me this entire story as having happened in oh, Montana or someplace in California involving a small-town banker, I'd picture Porter in my mind's eye as you're talking."

"The whole scheme, us stealing those stocks, was supposed to cover up the theft of the people's savings."

"So it seems."

"I'm framed. I'm in a box."

"You need my help. Well, I don't know as I can help you any, but I do know someone who might. Are you acquainted with Judge Ira Parfrey?"

"No, ma'am. I don't know anybody in Goodnight, except the Fairchilds."

"That's a pity. It's a nice town, nice, decent, hard-working people. That's what makes it so difficult to believe they'd lynch a man, for stealing at any rate."

"Their hard-saved money?"

"Even that. If he'd killed a child, if he'd raped—"

"I'm afraid it don't take much to turn nice people into a mob with blood in their eyes."

She got up and began pacing. "If you and I met with Ira—"

"Excuse me, ma'am. I couldn't go into town."

"Of course not. We'll have to get word to him, get him out here. He's retired, but still highly respected around these parts. He's honest, fair-minded. He could advise you as to your next move. And, I hope, what can be done about Porter Fairchild." She paused and looked at him. "Is something bothering you?"

"I don't know. The more I think about it, a judge—that's like a sheriff or a marshal. If he advises me to give myself up he's gonna be barking up the wrong tree."

"I think that's the last thing he'll want you to do. Where were you planning to stay tonight?"

Slocum shrugged. "Anyplace I can find a bed."

"Stay here, in the guest room. We'll get Ira out here first thing in the morning."

"I wouldn't want to put you out, at this bad time and all."

"You won't be putting me out. You look tired, Mr. Slocum. You could use a good night's sleep."

"Thank you kindly, ma'am."

"Come, I'll show you to your room. Then we'll have a nice hot supper. Do you like beef stew?"

Slocum grinned. "Does a cat like cream?"

30

Shucking his clothes, he washed at the basin, chucked the dirty water out the window and slipped his naked body under the cool white sheet covered with a paper-thin blanket.

A comfortable bed. He bounced. Iron springs, feather pillow. This was class. Elbows high, hands behind his head, he studied the pink-globe Zenith lamp suspended from the ceiling directly overhead, trapping a beam of moonlight slanting in through the upper window. The room was small, big enough for the bed, a chest of drawers at the foot and a clothes cabinet alongside it filling the corner.

He thought about Alice Weatherly, feeling sorry for her. She was young to be losing her husband, left with a spread to run, bills to pay, a payroll to meet. Over the stew she had told him about Weatherly and his success in raising horses. He would box in a herd, drive them back, feed them, break them and sell them in lots. A tough business. Wild mustangs weren't like cattle, they couldn't be pushed around. They had spirit where livestock had none. Breaking spirit—in a horse, a man or a woman—was hard work and took time. Horses were no job for a lazy slouch.

His Alice had enviable spirit. Slocum could see she was taking his death hard, but with grit and a fatalism that rendered tears and complaining useless.

If Judge Ira Parfrey was all Alice Weatherly claimed, he could help him bust Porter Fairchild wide open. She didn't like Porter; the judge probably shared her sentiments. If he could just get those damned wanted dodgers pulled down and thrown away, or better yet a strip added to them, angling across saying: "Not Guilty!"

Then maybe the accused could shave. Damned red bush itched, furiously when he sweat. It was probably the dye, he thought. There was one other thing he didn't much cherish about going red: it reminded him of Jay Packer. And he didn't enjoy the sadness that thoughts of Jay inspired. The brothers Fairchild would pay in spades for all their sins, but for what they'd done to Packer they would pay with their hides!

A timid knock. "Are you decent?"

He pulled the sheet and blanket an inch farther up, touching his neck. "Come in."

She appeared with a cup of coffee, steaming hot. "Fresh made, I thought you might like a cup."

"You bet. It'll really hit the spot."

She set it on the night table. "Better let it cool a bit before you drink it."

She was dressed for bed in a mother hubbard, the square-cut neck framing the perfect pink flesh of her throat. Richly embroidered, the mother hubbard was dotted with ribbon bows and showed mammoth puff sleeves that became slender down her forearms to her wrists. Her breasts, outlined under the thin material, amazed him. They were huge compared to what he'd seen earlier when she was fully dressed. No longer flattened, they stood forward majestically, the nipples hard against the material, aroused by the gentle scraping of it as she moved her arms.

She lit the night-table lamp and set it on the chest of drawers at the foot of the bed. Standing in front of it talking to him, the orange light outlined her lovely figure, her slim waist, her hips. The beautiful view was in no way a play for his attention, however. There was nothing suggestive, nothing sensual or intimate in what she said. She talked about Porter Fairchild only, rambling on about her dealings with him over the years. Propped up listening, looking at her and nodding, Slocum could feel tiny beads of perspiration start from his forehead, his neck and under his arms.

Her eyes, her skin, her body, the soft music of her voice, the tone matter-of-fact though it was, began getting to him. The Widow Weatherly. The door shut, the rest of the ranch fast asleep, only the moon and the lamp looking on—. He felt his cock awake and begin tingling slightly as it filled. Staring, listening, nodding, he began stripping her in his mind, pulling her slowly down upon him so that she could feel his hardening cock pressed flat against her firm flawless stomach.

"Mr. Slocum, you're perspiring."

"Yeah, it is a mite hot in here."

"It's that blanket. It's so thin you can practically see through it but I declare it's warmer than a horse blanket. Here."

Her hand shot out stripping the blanket clear to the foot. She began folding it, avoiding sight of his half-hard cock beginning to elevate the sheet. He rolled over on his side to conceal it. All at once he felt like a fool kid unable to control himself. Unable to stop sweating, his heart thudded in his chest, his balls filling like two rain barrels in a deluge.

"Maybe I shouldn't have brought you hot coffee. Would you rather some cold lemonade?"

"No, that's okay."

"I can make it in a jiffy." She came around the corner of the bed, her slender hands gripping the knob, her great breasts swinging with a soft rushing sound under her gown.

"The coffee's fine, thanks."

"Here." She pulled the sheet down to his waist. "I'll open your window, too. It's close in here. It's such a tiny room."

"Yes, ma'am, close—tiny—"

He sipped the coffee. It was excellent, the best he'd had since Dr. Talleyborough's. It made his own trail coffee taste like dirty poison. She had returned to the foot of the bed, the light continuing to outline her figure. Slocum lay on his left side, his cock gigantic, pulsing like a runaway tumbling rod on a spur jack, silently roaring for action, urged on by his drumming balls. He groaned in his heart.

"Well, I guess I'd better leave you alone so you can get some sleep," she said. She covered a yawn delicately, fastidiously, and smiled. "My gracious, I'm getting sleepy myself. Good night, Mr. Slocum, sweet dreams. If the breeze comes up during the night, don't be reluctant to close the window. Sometimes the wind changes and blows in with a blast."

"Yes, ma'am. Good night, and thanks again for the coffee." Draining the cup, he handed it to her.

She left.

31

Judge Ira Parfrey filled his clothes to such a tightness that he appeared ready to snap the buttons. Round and rosy, his chins stacked up under his mouth like layers of rolled dough. And the—by his own admission—275 pounds upholstered to his bones exuded sweat in steady profusion, rendering his shirt wringing wet and staining his celluloid collar yellow around the upper edge.

But Slocum liked him—his laugh, his steady eye, his forthright manner, his patience as a listener. The three sat in the kitchen over flapjacks and second coffee. At

Alice Weatherly's urging, Slocum had related the events of the past weeks and the Fairchild brothers' actual and presumed part in them.

The Widow Weatherly—her lovely breasts returned to disillusioning and depressing incarceration under a full-figure corset—looked cool and attractive. Her hair was fixed in a bun, her pretty smile in evidence, her slender hands gestured animatedly. She backed up Slocum's every assertion with enthusiastic comment. The stock certificates were the key, thought Slocum. What better device to prove his sincerity than handing them over. God bless Rip Ripley's brains! Everything was going beautifully, right up to the finish of the story of John Slocum. At which point Judge Ira Parfrey detonated his bomb.

"I see only one problem," he said. "Porter."

"Surely there's sufficient evidence to bring charges," said Mrs. Weatherly. "Can't the law demand to look into his holdings, his finances? If he stole the twenty-two thousand, and it's obvious he did, surely he's invested it. Can't that be checked?"

"I'm sure it can," said the judge. "The trick is to find the man. I'm sorry to say I think he's left town. Under the circumstances, probably for good."

Slocum felt his jaw drop. Jesus Christ, he might have known!

"You know for a fact he's gone?" asked Mrs. Weatherly.

"I didn't say that, I said I think. I've been in the bank three or four times this week and there's no sign of him. And Alice, you know Porter, he practically eats and sleeps there."

"Maybe he's gone on vacation," she said, glancing at Slocum with a sympathetic look.

"He's flown the coop," Slocum said. "What about his brother?"

"Still around, far as I know," said the judge.

Slocum pounded the table, jiggling his empty cup on its saucer. "Great! Let's get a collar around him and start pumping him. He'll know everything we got to, including where Porter's run off."

"All well and good," said the judge, "only how do you propose to 'collar him'?"

"Easy. Get him out here with some cock-and-bull story, disarm him and go to work. Mrs. Weatherly, did I hear you say he's been out before, looking into trouble?"

"Yes, a fight. One of the men shot a stranger passing through. As I recall, one accused the other of stealing. Seth disarmed the two of them and sent a man in for Tyson. He rode out and arrested the guilty one."

"Then that's it," said Slocum.

"That's what?" she asked mystified.

"We'll set a trap for him, maybe pull the pins out of the corral-gate hinges. Make out a band o' rustlers hit the place last night and made off with your herd. Get him out here to look around, ask questions, the usual."

She nodded. "I'll send one of the men into town at once." She got up. "You'll stay, won't you, Ira?"

The judge beamed. "I wouldn't miss this for the world."

"Wait just a shake," cautioned Slocum. "Let's figure how we're gonna handle it before he walks in the door. Red hair or not he's gonna recognize me in two seconds."

"Why don't you stay in the bedroom until you hear him come in?" she suggested. "We'll get him in here and demand to know where Porter is."

Slocum shook his head. "He'll never let on. Why should he? How do you figure to make him? No, I'll hide in the bedroom, all right, but only to get the drop on him. We'll have our hands full unless I get his gun."

Judge Parfrey looked glum. "Now it's beginning to get a bit complicated. What's your idea, Slocum, back him up against the wall and beat it out of him?"

"No sir. There'll be no need to lay a hand on him."

She nodded. "He's right, Ira. Tyson's into this business as deeply as Porter. If we make him see that it's in his best interest to talk—"

"He'll spill his guts," said Slocum. "Maybe not to us, Judge, but you sure can put the fear o' God into him."

"We'll see," said Judge Parfrey. "But Alice, I think you'd better stay out of it. It could get hot and heavy."

Slocum nodded agreement. "One of us might, you know, take the Lord's name in vain or something."

32

Judge Parfrey sat in the parlor, rocking aimlessly, his fat pink hands folded under his watch chain, a twisted black cheroot occupying the corner of his mouth. Slocum sat in an adjoining bedroom, the door an inch ajar, allowing him to see the front door. They waited and waited and waited some more, Slocum now and then going out into the parlor to talk to the judge, then returning to his hiding place.

It was nearing sundown when a knock sounded at the door. Heaving his bulk out of his chair, the judge winked at Slocum, signaled silence and going to the door, eased it open a few inches.

"Tyson, come in, come in."

"Judge, what are you doing here?"

He took off his hat and looked around. Slocum bit his lip, his hand going for his .44, tightening on the grip. How he'd love to bushwhack the bastard, put four clean through his pot belly and drop him where he stood! The murdering son of a bitch!

"Where's Alice at? What's all this about mustang rustling?"

Drawing, Slocum pulled the door open, leveling his weapon at Tyson.

"What in hell—" began the sheriff.

"Get his gun, judge," said Slocum. With surprising swiftness for a man of his bulk, the judge closed on

Tyson, snatching his .45 from its holster. Slocum held out his hand, taking the gun from the judge. Tyson was staring at him, the light of recognition filling his eyes.

"You, Slocum. Judge, this man is wanted for robbery and murder!"

"Just shut up and take a chair, Tyson," said the judge.

"You didn't hear me! Slocum, you're under arrest. Hand over the guns, come on!"

"I said sit!" snapped the judge and to Slocum's surprise pushed the sheriff down hard into the rocker he had been occupying.

"Judge, have you got any idea what this mangy bastard has done, the crimes he's committed?"

Judge Parfrey leaned over and bellowed in his face. "Shut your mouth!"

Holstering his gun, Slocum approached Tyson, standing over him, arms folded, staring down contemptuously. The judge took another chair across from the sheriff.

"Where's Alice?" demanded Tyson. "Get her in here."

"Never mind Alice," said Slocum. "If it's them railroad stocks on your mind, don't worry, she's got 'em back, every one. We got a question for you. Where's Porter?"

"Search me."

"He's left town, right?"

"I don't know. I don't live with him, I'm not his keeper."

"Okay, you want to play games, let's lay out the rules. Let's see where you stand, Mr. Lawman. You and him stole the money long before he put me and Turnbull and Jay Packer onto stealing the stocks. Count one against you. Count two, you left Packer's cell door open so's the mob could get at him. Your job is to protect prisoners so they can be brought to trial. But a trial was the last thing you and Porter wanted, right? First send me chasing off after the wild goose, then get rid o' poor old Jay. Count three—"

"That's enough, Slocum," said the judge. "I think

he gets the point. Tyson, you know what you've been up to. And so do we."

"You can't prove a goddamned thing, Ira. If my brother did anything illegal, that's between the law and him. Me, I'm as innocent as a newborn babe. I just do my job day by day, upholding the law."

"You're a fuckin' liar!" barked Slocum. "Flooding the landscape with them dumb wanted dodgers, five thousand dollars' reward! Christ Almighty, you had the damned things printed up six hours after I left Goodnight, just waitin' to hear from me before you sent 'em out! I was supposed to run right back with the stocks, let you toss me back into a cell and hand me over to the mob like you did Packer. And when you got my telegram you contacted the sheriff in Seminole asking about Turnbull. When he wired back Turnbull had been shot you couldn'ta been happier. And when I didn't show you started scattering dodgers like fuckin' corn in a hen yard. You already had two of us dead. Get rid o' the third and you and Porter'd be in the clear."

"You been chewing *peyote*, cowboy. Your head is fulla dreams."

"You claim otherwise?" inquired the judge.

"I claim he's fulla shit!"

"That's just the way it worked, Judge, step by step," said Slocum. "It doesn't take no crystal ball to figure it out."

"It shouldn't be too hard to prove. The twenty-two thousand dollars you and Porter claim Slocum here and his friends stole. If that's so, where's the money now?" The judge eyed Tyson steadily.

"How am I supposed to know?" asked the sheriff. "Maybe Turnbull hid it."

The judge paid no heed. He was too engrossed in linking the pieces together. "On the other hand," he went on, "if we check into Porter's investment pattern these past few weeks and it shows sudden activity; if the bartender at the saloon in Prayerville testifies that Porter made the acquaintance of Slocum and the other two the way Slocum here claims; if Porter can't be found to testify in his own behalf and yours; if we're able to track down the handful of roughnecks you paid to rile up the lynch mob that hanged Packer; if I can turn up a witness who'll admit Packer's cell door was unlocked when he was taken, or that you failed to hide the keys as any decent law officer would have done when things looked to be getting out of hand—"

"If, if, if," snarled Tyson. "If a Christmas tree was a fuckin' cow, it'd give milk."

"A good deal more than if," said the judge icily. "You happen to be in a great deal of trouble, Tyson, for which you can thank your dear brother. Complicity in bank robbery, complicity in murder, complicity in attempted murder, accessory to fraud. Tyson, you can get ten years. Ten years in Rusk or Huntsville. Not much of a choice, I'm afraid. I'll wager you've arrested at least fifty men who've wound up behind one set of bars or the other."

"They're gonna be happier than pigs in shit seeing you walk in," added Slocum. "There's nothing like renewing old friendships."

It was the right tack. Tyson squirmed in his seat, not much, just enough to indicate that discomfort was setting in. The color faded in his cheeks, and he sent the tip of his tongue riding across his lower lip, proof that his mouth was drying.

The judge picked up the play. "I know a lawman who was caught with his fingers in the pie and got sent up for three years. Huntsville, unless I'm mistaken. Marshal Lydell Kennedy. Name sound familiar?"

"Never heard of him," said Tyson, his eyes flashing from one to the other.

"They say his first month inside he got into twenty-five fights. Spent most of the time in the infirmary, poor man. All for arresting a fellow who'd robbed some express office and pocketing half the money in exchange for letting him go. They couldn't prove Kennedy shot him, so he got off with three years.

"The other prisoners made it so hard for him at Huntsville he was transferred to Rusk. From the frying pan into the fire. They put excrement in his food. They urinated in his coffee. He got into a fight and was placed in solitary confinement for thirty days. One little window high up the wall in a five-by-five cell. Somebody dropped two buckets full of live rats through the window."

"You bastards—" He could mouth aggression and profess unconcern, but he was having a hard time concealing his true feelings. As lurid as the picture sketched by the judge may have been, Tyson knew, as did Slocum, that it was true.

"On the other hand," said the judge, "you tell us where Porter is and agree to cooperate all the way down the line and you may never have to see the inside of either of those friendly, homey institutions." The fat man leaned over, bringing his round red face to within two inches of Tyson's. "Make up your mind, Tyson, what'll it be?"

"Goddamned greedy bastard! I told him and told him! You can't do it, I said. You can't take on the whole damned town! He wouldn't listen, never does. Stubbornest son of a bitch in the whole entire world, that's him. He knows, nobody else knows shit!"

"Where is he?" asked Slocum.

"Down the coast."

"Where down the coast?"

"Near Aspinwall."

Slocum stared at the judge inquiringly.

"Down below Houston," said the judge. He grinned at Slocum over Tyson's bowed head, the sheriff's words addressed to the rug at his feet.

"What's so interesting down in Aspinwall?" asked the judge. "Speak up, Tyson. Don't make us pull it out of you."

"Oil! Oil! He's got a couple wells down there. He's poured every cent we have in the world down 'em. Oh Christ, I was dead against it from the first. I told him tear the fuckin' money up and throw it into the sea, but don't go into oil. It has to be the worst goddamned gamble in the world!"

"Poured *your* money into the wells, then the depositors'," said the judge, "is that it?"

Tyson nodded. All the fight had gone out of him. He raised his eyes, the look of the lost taking hold, the look of a man thoroughly beaten and disturbingly aware of it.

"These past few weeks he's been like a crazy man. He actually wanted me to hire a bunch and us go out and rob a bank!"

"You mean another bank?" said the judge.

Tyson nodded. "Prayerville, Coombs, Loomis, anywhere. Can you imagine? I mean that's how desperate he is."

"And the wells turned up dry," said Slocum.

"Like hell, that's the whole goddamned trouble. The first one went down beautiful, down to four hundred sixty feet and oil. Up it comes, three hundred barrels a day. For two whole days. Then it stops, just like a faucet shutting off. Paraffin."

Slocum and the judge stared questioningly. "Paraffin?" asked Slocum.

"The damned tubing got clogged up. The crew couldn't even drive an iron rod through it with sledgehammers. They tried live steam, acids, everything. Nothing. All that oil lying down underneath and plugged up like a cork in a whiskey bottle."

"Tsk tsk," said Slocum, "what a shame."

"What about the other well?" asked the judge.

"Oh Christ, everything in the world's gone wrong with that son of a bitch! First the water petered out and there wasn't enough to drill with, then a gas explosion ruined nearly a thousand bucks' worth of pipe. They hit quicksand that couldn't be circulated with three pumps, all the power we got! Bad as the damned paraffin in the other well. They finally cleared the hole and she started pumping. Two hundred barrels a day at five hundred feet. Then a cave-in and more quicksand plus a windstorm comes along and blows down the derrick. I told him. I talked to him like a Dutch uncle. He wouldn't listen. He knows. He tossed our money and everybody else's down them holes like water!"

"I'm sorry I got drawers on," said Slocum.

"Huh?"

"I can't show you how much my ass is bleedin' for you."

"You don't understand, cowboy. We put everything we had into the thing, practically our life's blood."

"Two men are dead, and you wouldn't have stopped until you'd killed the third," said the judge.

"You can't pin any o' that on me. I haven't killed a soul, I swear to God. If anybody's dead, it's Porter's fault, not mine."

"What do you mean if?" asked Slocum. "Tell me about how Packer got it. That I want to hear."

"He was lynched."

"Explain all the gory details."

Tyson's voice took on a sheepish tone, his words mumbled, barely intelligible.

"Word got out we'd caught the bank robbers."

"Word got out?" asked Slocum. "You mean you let it out." Tyson shrugged. "Don't shrug me, you murdering son of a bitch. You let it out!"

"It was all Billy Janes, Judge," continued Tyson. "You know what a damned hothead he is. Man don't have a brain in his head. He come storming in with three or four of his friends, no big mob, just a handful."

"Was Packer's cell door unlocked, did you hand 'em the key, or did they take it down from the wall?" asked Slocum.

"They came burstin' in, surprised the shit outta me. Held a gun on me, took down the key ring, hauled him out and rode off with him."

"How much did it cost you?"

"Huh?"

"Don't 'huh' me, you bastard. I'm askin' how much it set you back!"

"Take it easy, Slocum," said the judge.

"Did you lay a fuckin' red carpet down from the cell to the front door?"

"Mister, I couldn't stop 'em. You got to understand I was alone, five against one. And they got the drop on me. I found out later they took him out on the Prayerville road and strung him to a tree."

"Knowing old Jay, he wouldn't go quietly. Did he stir up a big fuss? Did he call you down? How'd you feel watchin' him fight for his life? Did it make you happy? Did you laugh? Did you feel a big load off your mind?" Slocum was leaning over him, barking the questions at him, ignoring the judge's hand tightening on his left arm. Holstering his gun, he hauled off and smashed Tyson full in the jaw.

"Here, here." Judge Parfrey pulled him back. "That's not going to help matters."

"You rotten bastard! Greedy motherfucker! So help me God I'll see you and that fuckin' brother o' yours swing! I'll see the goddamned buzzards stripping you raw!"

Tyson rubbed his jaw gingerly. "You got it all wrong, cowboy. I didn't hang your friend. I was nowhere near there."

"Tyson," said the judge quietly, "for a lawman you are distressingly ignorant of the law. You hanged him just as if you'd slipped the rope around his neck and beat his horse out from under him. You're as responsible as Janes and the others. Which reminds me, I'll want all their names. You're going to have company where you're going."

"What are you talkin' about? You said you'd help me! Keep me outta jail! You promised!"

"What I said was, if you cooperate, you may never have to see the inside of Rusk or Huntsville. I made no ironclad promise. What happens to you is up to judge and jury."

"I'll deny every fuckin' word! I'll get up on the stand and swear to God on the Bible I had no part in any of it!"

The judge nodded. "You do that." He lowered his voice, filling it with menace. "And I'll see you hang. *That*, Tyson, is an ironclad promise."

"When's that bastard brother o' yours coming back?" asked Slocum. "Is he?"

"Answer him, Tyson!" snapped the judge.

"You two got to be stupid as stone if you think he's comin' back here."

"He's right," said Slocum. "Why bother, he's already milked the cow dry."

Wagon wheels and horses sounded outside. "That's probably Alice coming back from her ride," said the judge. Going to the door, he opened it. She came in, dusting her apron with the ends of her shawl and glancing about. "What a relief," she said. "I envisioned this place in a shambles."

"Alice," said the judge," we'll need a couple of your hands to go with Mr. Slocum here. They'll be taking sheriff—that is Mr.—Fairchild in."

"Where?" asked Slocum.

"Loomis. I know the marshal there. I'll go along with you and explain the situation. Between us we might make some semblance of sense out of it. We'll have to keep our friend here under wraps until Porter's brought back. Anyone of half a dozen charges will do to hold him."

"I favor murder," said Slocum.

"Let's get started, Tyson."

The sheriff rose, scowling. "You know what you're doin', Ira, takin' the law into your own hands."

"Indeed I am. I'd say it's high time somebody around here took it out of yours!"

Slocum snickered and followed the two of them out the door. Mrs. Weatherly lay a hand on his shoulder.

"You'll come back, won't you?"

"I don't know whether I can."

"You've still got two days until your friend from Humble City gets here."

"Yeah. I'd almost forgotten about old Rip." He nodded. "I'll be back."

"I'll turn down your bed."

Mounting his horse he waved and rode off with the others. Putting a very personal question to himself. Was he, he wondered, just naturally inclined toward the sort of self-made misery that seemed to flourish in the little bedroom?

33

"That mother hubbard sure wasn't after your bone, you dog!" Ripley laughed, beat the table, threw half a shot of rye past his teeth and refilled his glass. Across from Slocum in the Palace Bar in Prayerville, he had been listening in undisguised fascination to John's account of his experiences of the past three nights under the Widow Weatherly's roof.

"I never have seen a woman like her," said Slocum in a defeated tone. "She got it, she shows it, sticks it right under a man's nose, then pulls it back like you'd tease a kid with a stick o' candy."

"And you still claim she doesn't know what she's up to? That it's all innocence, that she's just being friendly, never dreaming she's getting you all hot and bothered? Slow-come, you got to be losing your grip!"

"It's the bald truth, dammit all! As far as she's concerned I might just as well have nothing but nothing between my legs!"

Again Rip laughed. "Is that the problem?"

"It ain't funny! I get so fuckin' hot I like to blow the sheet clear off the bed!"

"So after the first night how come you went running back for more? Three nights in a row. Hell, you must be climbing the walls."

Slocum sighed. "I went back 'cause I figured I could score," he said glumly.

"You can't score if you can't get the game started."

"I'll tell you the truth. I'm afraid to touch her. I'm afraid it'd shock her so, she'd be liable to have a stroke."

"Balls, you're just fishing for alibis. Why would she set the light behind her but to show off her equipment under old mother hubbard?"

"That's what I'm trying to explain to you, she don't know she's showing it off! Only reason she moves the light is to get it outta the way o' the conversation."

"Sure."

"That's so, dammit!"

"How long since her man died?"

"About a week. And he was sick before that. It wouldn't surprise me none if she hasn't been plugged in a couple months. I tell you, Rip, I been up and down the territories fifteen years. I fucked 'em all: short, tall, light, dark, clean, dirty, drunk, sober. I been chewed by more goddamned mouths than a Cheyenne peace pipe. I can spot a frustrated woman, a hot one, a cold one, all the kinds there is, six miles away. But her I can't figure for sour apples! All I know for sure is if anything's gonna happen she's got to make the first move."

"Dummy, she's made it, putting that light behind her, turning the sheet down to your waist."

"She don't know what she's doing to me. If you were there, if you saw, you'd say the same thing."

"There's one way to solve the problem."

"Yeah?"

"I'll borrow a razor and lop your dick clean off. Then you can move in permanent and no sweat."

"You're a goddamned barrel o' laughs, you know that?"

"So the schoolmarm said. Seriously, though, if it was me I'd give that place a five-mile-wide berth. Get your ashes hauled here in Prayerville or someplace 'round about. And forget her."

"I can't. And getting laid ain't gonna solve nothing. That'd be just temporary relief. I got to have her!" The line-up at the bar turned in unison, gaping. Slocum lowered his eyes over his rye. "Son of a bitch!"

"Why don't we change the subject," said Rip.

"I get pins and needles all over!"

"Tell me about this sheriff you got locked up over to Loomis."

"He talked, just like the judge and me figured. But when we mounted up and rode away from the Weatherly spread he shut up quicker'n a Newhouse trap. Not a peep outta him. But get this, once we locked him in, he starts in spouting again."

"You said something about Aspinwall."

Slocum nodded. "Down on the Gulf. I've never been near the place, have you?"

"I been around there. It's oil country, all right. Did he tell you the names of the wells?"

"Welcome One and Welcome Two. The way I figure it we head on down, make inquiries, locate brother Porter, snatch the bastard, haul him back and turn him over to the judge."

"You're gonna need a warrant."

"Parfrey's getting it for me, some friend o' his . . ."

"One of us got to be deputized."

Slocum showed the deputy badge taken from Turnbull's brother-in-law. "The marshal in Loomis has already swore me in. Don't worry, I ain't about to let that thieving bastard get off the hook by some dumb screw-up."

"Don't figure to take him easy. He'll kick up a fuss. And working two wells, he'll have at least six or eight guns on his side." Rip pushed aside the bottle, then his half-filled glass, and fixed Slocum with a serious look. "And besides those working for him, he's bound to have buddies. Another thing, it's gonna be strange territory down there for us two."

"What's the matter?" burst Slocum, "you gettin' butterflies?"

"Hell no. I'm just pointing out that we got our work cut out for us."

"I know that. Christ Almighty, you think I'm stupid?"

"Now and then, yeah. How about with the widow?"

"We're offa that subject. Would you mind we stayed off?" Slocum paused, surveying Ripley with a critical eye. "You don't have to come, you know. I can go it alone."

"Shit, you do and you'll walk into a hornet's nest. I didn't come all the way from Humble City to see the beauties o' Prayerville, which everybody here seems to do a great old job o' hiding under wraps."

"I'm serious, Rip. You could get your ass shot off. How long's it been since you held a pistol? How rusty are you?"

"Don't you worry about this old boy."

"I'm glad to see you got outta that riverboat gambler outfit. And got yourself some decent duds."

"Never mind what I wear, what I look like, whether I can still shoot. You just be grateful there's still somebody around dumb enough to give you a hand. When do we leave?"

"What's the matter with right away?"

"Fine with me, right after you give your hair and face a once-over."

Slocum's hand went to his face. "What's the matter?"

"You're starting to show black roots. Dorabelle gave you what was left o' that red dye, didn't she?" Slocum nodded. "So find a mirror and touch yourself up."

"Stuff burns like a branding iron."

"Just grit your teeth like a big boy. You start looking like your wanted picture again and sure as hell we'll get stopped on the way."

Slocum nodded. "That's the goddamned trouble with wanted dodgers. They can paper the world with 'em in two days flat. But it takes six weeks to get 'em all taken down."

"Stop bellyaching. This thing's starting to turn

around. Be thankful. Fix your fur, then we'll get us that warrant and head out."

Slocum smiled. "I purely appreciate you're riding with me, Rip. You know I do. All I can say is I'd do the same for you if the saddles were switched."

"I know. Don't go getting all dewy-eyed and sentimental on me, for Christ's sakes. Hell, I'm gonna enjoy this. It's gonna be a regular vacation. Being a big business tycoon can get awful boring. Fella can get into a godawful rut."

"Screwing people, conniving, bullshitting the other barrel bellies, totaling up your ill-got gains, yelling down your conscience day in—"

"Oh shut up!"

34

An air of excitement, of nervous anticipation, characterized Aspinwall and the area surrounding it. Derricks cluttered the landscape. Some wells were in production, pumping 100 to 5000 barrels a day. Others had dried up, and not even torpedoing them with nitroglycerine could restore their flow. Down came their derricks and the entire rig, uprights, ties, braces, sills, everything was piled onto wagons and moved to another location.

But it was the third category that inspired and excited the hands: wells on the verge—at least in the minds of their drillers and tooldressers—of blowing and hurling an enormous black fountain into the sky. Oil would then rain down upon the earth, gravity pulling back the black gold stolen from the depths, reclaiming what it could before the well was capped, the gusher tamed, the barreling begun.

"What a filthy fuckin' place," observed Slocum with typical candor. Inhaling somewhat hesitantly, he sniffed and spat. "Christ, it's in the goddamned air, you can taste it!"

"You'll get used to it," Ripley assured him. He swept

the landscape with a glance. "They're so close some of 'em look like they're standing inside others. There must be five or six hundred."

"I wonder how many are making money?"

"Friend, they wouldn't be here working like mules 'round the clock, busting their balls, breathing this stinking air, risking arms and legs and lives if somebody wasn't making money."

"Old Porter ain't," said Slocum, "at least so his brother claims. I wonder which are his two?"

Ripley dismounted, pulled at the cheeks of his ass and stretched his legs. "We're gonna have to ask around."

"I hate doing that. We'd be tipping our hand for sure."

"We can play tricky. There's got to be some central location where wells and sites are written down in a book, otherwise everybody'd be at everybody else's throats. We could make out like we're buyers."

"We don't much look like buyers," said Slocum. "You'da been better off keeping that outfit you was wearing when we met up, cane and all."

"Clothes don't mean beans," responded Ripley. "Bullshit's the key to success. Just you watch me in action."

It was noon, the sun suspended directly overhead, blazing furiously, hurling its heat down upon the area, dazzling the eye so that Slocum was prompted to pull his hat brim down to his lids. It was time for the shift change on the working wells and those under the drill. Exhausted, grime-smeared men came trooping in from the fields, heading for one or the other of the two saloons facing each other down across the road. Few women were seen. It was no place for women or children or anyone who wasn't involved in drilling, barreling, selling or buying crude. The two waterholes were the best-looking buildings on the street. As far as Slocum could see, every other structure, from rooming houses to stable, displayed total neglect. Those in charge must have recognized the futility of trying to keep their property spruced up, painted and free of the black skin deposited by the breeze off the Gulf.

They took a room in the Wildcat, a roominghouse of no mean reputation according to the talkative old man sweeping the mud trackings into a corner of the hallway before shoveling them out into the front yard.

"I've been in Concord coaches bigger than this," commented Ripley, eyeing the room assigned them.

"Like the man said, nothing but the best," said Slocum.

The washbowl and pitcher were riddled with cracks, the window curtains stained and filthy, as if the previous occupants had dipped their hands in oil and wiped them. The double bed resembled a concrete slab. One window was broken, the entire upper frame removed, allowing the stink of crude entry. And a regiment of rats was busy holding maneuvers inside all four walls.

"Home sweet home," said Slocum. "Jesus, I wouldn't wish this shithole on them hogs I slopped back at the Double-H."

"With any luck we'll be outta here tomorrow night," said Ripley. "Do you suppose there's such a thing as a hot meal in this lovely town?"

According to the hallway sweeper, the Petrolia Café was the best restaurant in town. Sitting down at a table and looking around, Slocum wondered what the worst looked like. The place was packed with workers, stiff-suited business types and painted whores. Two waiters, one lame, covered 40-odd tables, scurrying about like fleeing thieves, dumping barely burnt beef, beer and booze before the diners. Everyone seemed to be talking at once, laughing, gorging themselves, rattling silver and china. Three men in overalls, greasy caps and plow boots sat at the next table hunched over their plates.

"They shot her and she was pumping over five hundred barrels an hour from two o'clock to four. By the end of the first twenty-four hours she'd got up close to ten thousand!"

"Horseshit!"

"It's the truth, so help me. It was like the whole field was pouring out one single well, flowing down the hill."

"That's so, Lucas, I heard."

"The casing head was on and the tools with the oil saver hung in the derrick, but they couldn't get men to go in. The foreman, feller named Watts, tried to get the tools down the hole, but the gas knocked him out and he fell under the bull wheels."

"Was he killed?"

"Damn near. The owners offered three hundred dollars to any man could turn the oil into the tanks. Me, Eddie Franklin and big Wiszcalski took a stab. We tied the packer for the oil saver on at the bull wheel shaft, set the tools over the hole and run in. But when we got the cap down to within a couple feet of the casing head, the pressure of the solid stream of oil against it was so powerful we couldn't get her down any lower. There she hung, two thousand pounds of tooling, the oil just holding it up like a feather floating over a gas jet."

"What did you do?"

"Wiszcalski got ahold of two long levers, and we put one on each side of the oil saver. Then we fixed the ends to one side of the derrick and applied pressure to the other ends, forcing the cap slowly down into position. Once down we turned the set screws on it. By this time that pressure was up close to three thousand pounds.

"There was a casing connection and tubing lines connecting the well with the gas tank. Two gushers of oil shot up through the gas escapes at the top. Up they went higher than the derrick. In no time the whole entire area was under half a foot of yellow crude. The trees got so loaded with it branches were bending down to the ground. It was like the earth was spewing up every last drop in her belly!"

Slocum cocked his head and stared at Ripley. "Sounds like a goddamn fish story to me." He glanced over the heads of the three men to the crowded tables beyond. A well-dressed man was standing, waving a handful of papers announcing leases for sale: sixteenth and thirty-second shares. He began disposing of them to two eager customers, and immediately three other men were on their feet waving leases, shouting prices. In thirty seconds the place turned into a madhouse, people shouting, pushing about, hands high, waving money and leases.

"Let's get outta here!" yelled Ripley above the din. "I'm getting a headache."

"What about our food?"

Ripley was on his feet. "To hell with it. This is no place to eat. Any second now, somebody's gonna start shooting. This is worse than a damn corral. Come on."

He was right. They were halfway out the door when the sound of loud cursing, a chair coming into contact with somebody's head and a roar of pain were heard. The entire dining room was galvanized to action. Reaching the plank street, Slocum and Ripley crossed it, turned and watched through the wide-open restaurant doors. Chairs careened about, fists cracked against bone, women screamed, men roared, six-guns barked, plates and steaks smashed against walls and diners, bottles shattered, tables collapsed.

"This whole damn town is nuts," observed Slocum. "Damned undertaker's got to be making more money than anybody!"

"The quicker we get outta here the better," commented Ripley. "I don't much fancy getting my head stove in by some crazy nitwit I haven't even been introduced to."

"I wonder where the sheriff is?"

"He's locked himself in his office if he's got any sense. I'm still hungry. Let's try one of the saloons."

"I wonder where 'bouts Fairchild is," said Slocum. "There's got to be five thousand people in this town. Be like looking for a needle—"

"We find his wells, we find him," said Ripley.

"I wouldn't want to go out there looking for him."

"The man's got to sleep someplace. Probably here in town. Might even be where we're staying."

Slocum nodded. "Unless he's got a cot in one o' his pumphouses. Or a cabin close by. No."

"No what?"

"That wouldn't be classy enough for him. He wouldn't want to chance getting his britches dirty."

"I'd like to know how he keeps 'em clean," said Ripley. "As far as I can see, the damned town's as dirty as the fields."

They went into the Old Glory Gambling Casino, which proved to be almost as crowded as the restaurant, with off-shift field hands, whores and waitresses, speculators, lease dealers, self-proclaimed capitalists, prospective investors, slick promoters, fortune-hunters, adventurers, troublemakers, rich men and poor men. Eight-inch-wide planks lay double-lined atop barrels with broken staves forming a bar running from the entrance to the back wall. Shelving and wooden cases behind the bar revealed hundreds of unlabeled bottles. Patrons stood elbow to elbow three deep at the bar, and an impressive array of gambling equipment spread wall to wall across the rear attracting as many people with faro, craps, three-card monte, thimble-rig and chuck-a-luck.

Slocum took one look and grinned. "Look at the crew running the games. Every one's a slick tinhorn. Look at that tall fella with the curly-brimmed derby hat and the red cravat with the diamond stickpin."

"Glass, I bet you."

The man who had drawn their attention was dealing three-card monte, his cards upheld lengthwise and slightly bent.

"Let's watch," said Slocum.

"Like hell. I'm hungry."

"So get us a couple sandwiches and meet me down there."

"Okay."

Ripley made his way toward the bar. Slocum pushed

through the crowd to the monte thrower. He watched, his right forearm held across his stomach against his money belt, almost as if he were afraid the man with the stickpin would reach out and pull it off him.

"Step up close, gentlemen, and watch me like a hawk. I have here three little cards: two red aces and the black queen of spades. The idea is very simple. All you have to do is find her ladyship. Find her and you win. Turn up an ace, you lose. What could be simpler? You're the hawk, I'm the pigeon. You can see my each and every move.

"Now remember, I take no bets from paupers, drunks or pregnant women. I show you all three cards, then throw them face down, fast—like so. If the hawk's eye is faster than the pigeon's and you spot the queen, I pay you the same amount you bet. I'll accept bets of five, ten, twenty, fifty or a hundred that you can't locate the lady. Remember, if you don't speculate you can't accumulate. No oil leases, no mortgages, no promissory notes, no checks, no Mexican money. U.S. money in hand or no bet. Here we go."

Slocum watched as the speaker got a player's bet down, manipulated the three cards swiftly and dexterously. The sucker stabbed his chosen card with his finger.

"That's her!"

The thrower revealed the ace of hearts.

"Sorry, friend, you lose. But you were close. I'll give you a chance to get even."

The fish swallowed the bait, hook and all, laid down a second five-dollar bill, locked his eyes to the fleetly moving cards and called the queen before all three came to rest.

Ace of diamonds.

"Tsk tsk tsk, another loser."

"Jesus Christ, your goddamned hands is faster than a rattler strikin'!"

"Next. Remember, if you don't speculate, you can't accumulate."

Ripley came sidling up with two ham sandwiches and two schooners of beer.

"You're not gonna bet, are you?" he asked Slocum warily.

"Just watching."

"Just keep on watching. There's no way you can beat a monte thrower. I found that out in Canyon City. My cellmate was a thrower. That was how he got thrown in. Even if by luck you put your hand on the queen he's got you. He'll take the money from a confederate, some guy betting on another card and because he says 'money in the hand or no bet,' you just plain don't have a bet when he sees you picked the winner."

They moved down the line to the chuck-a-luck.

"Good old sweat," said Slocum. "I think I'll give it a whirl."

"Step right up," yelled the dealer, "three winners and three losers every time."

Slocum reached for his money, but Ripley grabbed his wrist. "Hold off," he snapped irritably. "We come down here to find his nibs, not to waste time throwing money away. You can't beat any o' these games, and you know it. You've been burned a hundred times."

"I like gambling."

"You like losing."

"I've won plenty in my time."

"And dropped plenty more. Chuck-a-luck, craps, high dice, all of 'em no damned skill, all chance. Odds in favor o' the house every time. A man's got to be stupider than Abraham's ox to put hard-earned money up against dice."

"What hard-earned? I won it cheating at poker and you know it!"

"It's still hard-earned. It took you three hours, didn't it? It makes no sense, John, no sense at all. Better you piss your money away on liquor and whores than dice."

He was right and Slocum knew it, though the timely agreement of his conscience in no way diminished his yen to play. Nobody need remind him that dice were heartless and could only reduce the temperature of your hand. In a birdcage, in a cup, in a springbox, in somebody else's fist or his own he could never make 'em roll anyway but the way they wanted to. Poker and blackjack, rummy and pinochle demanded some skill, but not dice.

What made the damned things so enticing? he wondered. Was it because he knew deep down he'd wind up losing and the possibility he just might be able to stave it off was what started his nerves tingling and his heart banging his ribs? Or was it some kind of weak fiber in his character? Maybe the same kind of weakness that encouraged a man to finish off the last shot in a bottle when he knows from experience it's certain to tip him over the edge into blind drunkenness and split his head with a hangover.

Some people were born suckers, others developed the gift, but the most pathetic of all had to be those who realized they'd be taken but jumped right in regardless. Munching his sandwich and swigging his beer, he considered that breaking the dice habit had to be as tough as turning teetotaler—too damned jarring to the system to be worth the effort. But if here and now he summoned up every grain of willpower he possessed and concentrated on his sandwich and his beer, he could walk away from the cage.

"Come on, let's move around," Ripley said in Slocum's right ear.

John turned, to the sight of Ripley leaving the cage busily flattening three five-dollar bills and fitting them around his wad.

"You son of a bitch!"

Ripley's mouth stretched in a grin. "Now, now, only one play." Pocketing his money, he slapped Slocum on the back. "A little demonstration of the two secrets of success: knowing when to play, knowing when to quit."

"You double-faced bastard! Hypocrite fuck! All that goddamned sermonizing—"

Ripley laughed. They threaded through the tables making their way to the bar.

"I got an idea," said Slocum.

"That's gotta be worth more than a drink."

"Seriously, instead of asking around or even going into the fields, why don't we just camp outside and watch for him?"

"You could, you know what he looks like. But what if he's not around here? What if he's come and gone?"

On the verge of responding, Slocum caught himself, gulped, gaped and pointed.

"What's the matter?" asked Ripley.

"It's him, look."

Having reached the bar, Ripley turned, flashing a glance at the batwing doors. "The black *sombrero?*"

"That's him, big as day. Pompous son of a bitch, look at him! Let's get at him."

"You got your warrant?"

"Hot in my pocket. Come on."

Porter Fairchild stood in the doorway, his hands atop the open batwings surveying the crowd, as if looking for someone. Close to 50 feet and 100 bodies separated Slocum and Ripley from him. As they started toward him, Slocum in the lead, the crowd seemed to bunch up against the bar blocking their way, forcing them to circle wide to reach the doors.

Suddenly a shot shattered the loud babble, freezing the crowd. Slocum turned just in time to see the tall derby-hatted monte thrower grab his heart with both hands and sink out of sight. The crowd between Slocum and Ripley and the doors had also turned and immediately began surging toward the rear en masse, their mouths gaping with curiosity.

People in their way resisted the tide, standing fast, even, as Slocum and Ripley continued to push forward. The air was filled with insults, accusations and cursing, and scattered fighting erupted. Within seconds it became a full-scale brawl. Everybody appeared to be fighting everybody else, selecting the nearest available opponent.

A few made for the doors since vacated by Fairchild. But all their departure accomplished was to open things up, permitting freer swinging and introducing the furniture into the fray. Men roared, women screamed and the makeshift bar collapsed, prompting the line of drinkers to push forward and begin grabbing bottles. Ripley plunged into the struggle brandishing both fists, yelling and roundhousing. A surly, defiant-looking man obstructed his path. A hammer fist came out of nowhere, smashing Slocum in the side of the head, dizzying him momentarily, rousing his anger and triggering reprisal. Suddenly he remembered—

His nose!

He had to protect it. His eyes, his jaw, his guts, anything could take everything, but not his nose! Even a glancing shot could refracture the bone and spread the meat clear across his face. He held his left arm high protectingly, taking a shot in the forearm that nearly caused him to smash himself with his own upraised fist.

"Rip!"

"Yeah!"

"We gotta get outta this nuthouse!"

"No kidding." Ripley laughed sardonically.

He was, observed Slocum, applying the first and foremost injunction of brawling: giving better than he was receiving. Above the din came a loud splintering sound as a chair came down on top of a heavy-set party directly behind Slocum, dropping the man to his knees, a look of distress seizing his features. By now the bar was demolished. A wave of brawlers climbed over the fallen planks, bartenders and shattered barrels, smashing, drinking and stealing everything in sight.

Grabbing the top of his head with his left hand, Slocum stiffened his forearm in front of his nose, at the same time pounding away with his right, attempting to clear a route to the door. Unhampered by the need to protect himself, Ripley flailed away mightily, the crowd surrounding him giving way in the face of his whirlwind barrage. Then a table in the hands of two combatants came crashing down, slamming Rip full in the head and crumpling him to the floor. Miraculously, the blow failed to knock him out. Slocum pulled him to his feet and pushed him forward in the direction of the door.

By this time the hostilities had degenerated into a bloodbath. Crimson streams spattered and smeared faces and bald heads, fists and furniture. Somebody hurled a bottle that missed Slocum's head by inches, catching instead a seedy-looking field hand in the eye and popping the glass eye out of the opposite socket like a cork from a champagne bottle. The furniture destroyed in minutes, the battlers turned to barrel staves, the bar planks and bottles—full, empty, unbroken and broken. What had begun as a brawl and transmogrified into a bloodbath was now becoming indoor carnage. Slocum had never seen so many angry people jammed into such a relatively small space. But here they were on all sides, diligently and delightedly destroying one another.

It was get out or get killed. The craving for blood burned in every eye. Like a pack of wolves red-eyed and slobbering, fangs bared and gleaming, neighbor attacked neighbor, friend friend, stranger stranger, with no one save Slocum and Thorne Ripley giving thought to the door.

Shouldering and shoving, belting and bowling over, Slocum forced his way to within 15 feet of the entrance when the luck that had preserved his nose and the other vulnerable portions of his anatomy gave out. A gallon jug came crashing down on his red thatch. Out he went, floating away locked in the center of a vividly flashing purple star.

35

"Hold it against it!" insisted Ripley. "Here." Pushing Slocum's hand aside, he forced the piece of raw beef against John's left eye and set the heel of his hand against it. "If you get the goddamned swelling down, you'll be able to see."

Slocum closed his uninjured right eye, squinting through the black and blue puffed-up flesh surrounding his left one.

"Everything's hazy gray, like looking through dirty water to the bottom of a pool."

"Jumping Jesus, will you keep the meat against it like I told you?"

Slocum sat on the edge of the bed in the dingy room, Ripley towering over him tightening a blood-stained strip torn from the bed sheet around his right hand. Slocum's own free hand went to the top of his head, investigating the large lump produced by the jug.

"Ow."

"Shut up, stop bellyaching!"

"What in hell are you so pissed off about?"

"My goddamned gun hand feels like it's busted in sixteen places. It hurts like a son of a bitch!"

"Stop bellyaching. You think I got no pain? Christ, I'm hurtin' in sixty-five fuckin' places all over, even my damned heel! Man, did you ever in your life see a set-to like that?"

"Never. I've seen a herd stampede over a bunkhouse fulla trail hands that didn't do one-third the busting up that mob did."

"Half of 'em got to be dead. Got to be. Holy shit, whatta brawl!"

Ripley raised both arms. "It's this goddamned oil town. Everybody's all nerved up, high strung, waiting for the big gusher to come in, watching the other guy's pump up, hating him, green with jealousy. It's more than a contest, it's a fuckin' war. Nuts, everybody's nuts!"

"There he stood, the son of a bitch, hanging onto the doors, just waiting for my hand on his arm."

"With half the town between us and him. You notice he didn't stick around for the party. He had more sense."

"Sense your ass, it was all location. We couldn'ta got outta there with a damned team o' plow stallions. It was like a sardine can. What time is it?"

Ripley consulted his watch, winding it, listening to it, slipping it back into his pocket. "Almost midnight. You've been out cold for better than eight hours."

"Do tell. Jesus, no wonder I'm hungry."

"When you get your eye open, you can eat the steak. Me, I'm going to bed."

"Like hell." Slocum got up from the bed, continuing to hold the meat against his afflicted eye. "We got work to do. We can sleep after."

"What work? You think you're going after him this time o' night?"

"Best time of all."

"How do you figure that?"

"The work shifts change at noon and midnight, don't they?"

"So?"

"So he's likely heading out to his wells."

"What for? He doesn't do any dirty work. What would he be doing in the fields when he could be in bed?"

"If he's not there now, that's even better. We go out there, then sit and wait for him to show."

"I don't know. I don't much like going out among those hands. I've had enough o' them crazies tonight to last me six years. Besides, like I told you before, that's his backyard. Better we take him on neutral ground."

"Horseshit! I'm fed up fuckin' around, playing cat and mouse. We got no problem. He doesn't know you, and he won't recognize me, not 'til after I put the arm on him. I say we locate where his wells are at, ride on out, survey the site and take it from there. If he's not around, we'll sit tight and wait for him to show." He paused, lowering the meat, blinking and restoring it to position. "You know oil. How many men you figure he's got working for him?"

"Four, maybe six."

"That's not bad. Figure they divvy the day, that's two, maybe three."

"Yeah, but with what he's got hanging over his head he may have taken on a couple hired guns, bodyguards."

"I don't care!" snapped Slocum. "I don't care if he's got the whole goddamned Texas Rangers on his payroll!"

"I do!"

"Rip, it doesn't have to be hairy."

"It looks plenty fuckin' hairy to me. And the worst of it is just because we missed him back at the brawl, you got your ass up and you're spoiling to run off half-cocked as usual. If we're gonna play it, for Christ's sake let's play it cool!"

"All right, all right, cool, cool, ice-cold if you like."

"We can't go out with the idea of shooting it out. Kill him and you fuck yourself proper."

"I don't follow."

"Think, man. You need a written confession, a piece of paper signed and witnessed. His brother spilling the beans doesn't help you any. From what you told me back in Prayerville, it's this Porter who did all the stealing. You've got to get a written confession."

"Yeah. She said the same thing."

"Who?"

"That bounty hunter, Letty." He sighed. "Man, what a woman, what an appetite!"

"We catch him, ride him back to Loomis, lock him up and give him paper and pen."

"Right."

Buckling on their hardware they left the rooming house. Up the street a pale yellow light flooded out of the Old Glory Gambling Casino, but all appeared quiet inside.

"Let's have a look," suggested Ripley.

"Fuck it," said Slocum, lifting his hat and applying the raw meat to the bump on his scalp. "I don't care to see that shithole again as long as I live."

"Can I ask you something?"

"What?"

"What are you doing?"

"Trying to get the swelling down."

"Very good. Why in hell don't you bleed it with a cactus needle?" He scowled impatiently. "Will you put the damned thing back on your eye and keep it there?"

A couple passed by arm in arm, the man's hand covering his wife's affectionately. Slocum lowered his meat and tipped his hat.

"Excuse me, mister. I'm looking for a couple particular oil wells, the Welcome One and Welcome Two. Any idea where they might be?"

The man glanced at his wife, broke into a grin, and looked back at Slocum.

"Mister, you must be new in town. You're talking about the two biggest-producing wells in the entire field, maybe along the whole coast."

"Is that a fact?"

"I mean to say. Six or seven thousand barrels a day, that's the Welcomes. Unbelievable."

"Funny, I heard they'd both run into trouble, paraffin, quicksand, a windstorm taking down one of the derricks."

"Somebody's pulling your leg. You should only own a sixty-fourth share in either one."

"Where 'bouts are they?"

"Do you know the fields at all?"

"Not really."

The man pointed up the street. "Go all the way to the end where the planks stop. Turn left at the stable and head straight out about a mile. When you get out, look for the tallest derrick. That would be the Lady Pay."

"Right."

"She's taller by fifteen feet than any other derrick out there. Right behind her, a little to the left, you'll find Welcome One. Welcome Two's right behind her."

"Thank you, mister."

"Don't mention it."

36

The mile ride out was an experience for Slocum. The town stank of oil, particularly when the wind blew in off the gulf over the fields. Out here among the rigs, however, the odor was doubly powerful, setting his nostrils aching and building a rancid taste in his mouth, somewhat reminiscent of rotten licorice. The moon hung full, salt-white in the blue night. The stars glittered and gleamed and the breeze, despite the stench, was cool and welcome after the heat of the day. On all sides rigs pumped tirelessly, drawing the crude from the depths. Gas flames flowered, dotting the area with orange bursts. Workers busied themselves at a variety of jobs. Two men carried a crown block toward one derrick, two others uncoiled seagrass rope, preparatory, Slocum assumed, to looping it over the block wheel before raising it high. Smokepipes dotted engine-room roofs, belching white clouds upward into the darkness. The chorus of turning wheels and walking beams pushing back and forth came at them from all sides as they rode along.

"How do you figure to work this?" asked Ripley.

"I can't say 'til I see the setup. In this light, with any luck we'll be able to see who's out there and how many right off."

"Light works just as well for their eyes."

Slocum flung away the meat, blinking his eye jerkily. "Yeah, but they don't know we're coming, who we are, what we want. Jesus, Rip, you do have a bug up your ass, you know that?"

"I'm not overly smitten with this stinking battlefield. If it comes to a shoot-out, you can damned well bet the crews all around are gonna come running. Shooting first and asking no questions."

"We'll see."

"You bet we will."

They found the Lady Pay without any difficulty, approaching it from the north and sighting Welcome One through it.

"There seems to be one powerhouse working both pumps," observed Ripley. "See the two stacks, one at each end? Two power units."

"What's that shack on the other side, I wonder?"

"Tools, equipment and sleeping quarters, I bet."

Passing the Lady Pay and nearing the shack, Slocum could see two slender rods of light framing a shade over the near side window.

"Somebody's home. This is far enough," he added, lowering his voice. "We can walk it from here."

They dismounted, Ripley unbooting his Winchester. "How do you want to work it?"

"You lay back, belly down, and cover me. I'll go up and knock on the door. They open it, I'll get the drop on 'em."

"You better hope there aren't more than five or six."

"Why should there be a bunch this time o' night? The only thing I worry about is if anybody gets off a shot. Sure as hell it'll bring the neighbors."

"I'll keep 'em off your tail. Just don't shoot unless you absolutely got to."

"Tell them, not me."

Ripley dropped, his rifle at ready, his pistol on the ground within reach.

"Jumping Jesus!"

"What's the matter?"

"If you think the air stinks, you oughta smell the ground. I can hardly breathe."

"Sssssh."

Pinning the deputy badge over his pocket, Slocum took out the warrant and set his free hand on the grip of his .44. Coming up to the door, he knocked loudly.

"Yeah?" The voice inside was muffled, as if the speaker was talking through a yawn.

"Open up," said Slocum.

"Who is it?"

Standing back, Slocum raised his right leg and heeled the latch as hard as he could. The door sprang as easily as the door to Turnbull's room in the Bluebonnet House. Two men were seated at cards in front of a pot-bellied stove, a kerosene lamp sitting on a crate beside them.

Fairchild raised his hands slowly, staring in confusion. "Who are you? What's the meaning of this?"

"You're under arrest."

The other man standing behind Fairchild and slightly to the right went for his gun. He got it out and half up before Slocum fired, hitting his hand and sending the weapon clattering to the floor. Then everything happened at once.

Another man came running around the corner of the shack, Colt in hand. From out of the darkness behind Slocum came two quick shots, doubling over the new arrival and dropping him, but not before his pistol snapped off four wild shots in rapid succession. Pushing Fairchild back with his gun muzzle, Slocum entered the shack, slamming the door behind him.

"Keep 'em high, Fairchild. You—" He motioned to the other man. "On your feet."

"My hand, it's busted!"

"I warned you. Nobody told you to play hero." Slocum cast about, spying a lariat coiled over a chair. "Tie him up, Fairchild. Make it fast."

"Slocum. John Slocum." Fairchild's eyes widened.

"In the flesh."

"You're no deputy."

"Stop yakking and do like I tell you. Tie him!"

Fairchild complied, knotting the other man's hands behind his back and cross-tying his ankles.

"What are you trying to do, John?"

"What the hell do you think, I'm taking you in. We got your big brother, you make it the full set. You pulled me through the pipe, mister, six miles long. I figure you stole about five years off the end o' my life; my trigger finger's just itching to pull off and put you where you sent Jay Packer, so don't fuck with me."

"You have no authority."

Slocum waved the warrant. "It's all here, signed and legal. Now quit stalling and move!"

"You're not going to take me back, John. You're smarter than that." He pointed toward a double bunk in the corner. "There's a suitcase under that bunk with close to fifty thousand in it."

"Get it."

Fairchild got it. "Look."

"Don't open it, I believe you. You wouldn't lie, you never lie."

"It's yours, every penny. You want more, I'll get you more."

"Let's go. Bring it along."

"But—"

"Move!"

Outside, Slocum called to Ripley. "Bring up the horses. Rip? Rip?"

There was no response, no sound save the pumps round about, the musical clanking of tools and the murmuring breeze. Slocum pushed Fairchild ahead of him. Six steps and he stopped short. Ripley lay face down, his right cheek across his Winchester, his eyes huge and staring.

37

Slocum was no stranger to anger. He was capable of blowing bitter with the best, losing hold completely, busting heads, balls and blood vessels in short-fuse upheavals harrowing to behold. But it was something other than anger that rooted and began growing inside upon his finding Thorne Ripley dead. His jaw began to quiver, his hands tremble as he gripped Rip by the shoulder and rolled him over on his back.

"Rip—Rip—Rip," he whispered hoarsely. "Jesus God."

He could feel the fury mounting within, as if the blood in his veins and arteries was quickly coming to a boil, burning the wall flesh, his heart pulsing and pounding, his throat constricted, cutting off his breath. He gulped for air. Getting up he glanced about, a man suddenly disoriented, confused, seized and strictured by shock. Then he checked himself, raised his face to the heavens and roared, a soul-chilling howl that pulled the pain and frustration from him, emptying him. His shoulders slumped, his face angled downward, his arms dangled at his sides.

Closing Ripley's eyes, he stood for a long moment as workers gathered in a close circle, dirty-faced men mute and staring in bewilderment, in hostility. Slocum snatched up Ripley's rifle and swung it about, menacing them.

"Back off." He touched his star. "This man is under arrest." He flashed the paper. "Warrant. I'm taking him in."

Curling his finger around the trigger, he brought the muzzle up under Fairchild's chin and held it there.

"Take it easy, John. I didn't kill him."

"You want we should do anything, sir?" queried a voice out of the darkness.

"You do like I tell you or he's dead!" barked Slocum. "Just back off and make way. Do exactly as I tell you, Fairchild, or I'll blow your face off your head."

"Yes, yes—"

"Where's your horse?"

"Around back. I have a buckboard."

"Okay, pick him up, sling him over your shoulder."

"Mr. Clemans?" called a second voice.

Fairchild held up one hand commandingly. "It's all right, boys. This is a personal matter between myself and the deputy. Nothing serious, you can get back to work."

"Pick him up," said Slocum.

With some difficulty, Fairchild hefted Ripley over one shoulder. Slocum picked up the suitcase filled with money and collected the reins of his own and Ripley's horse.

"Lead the way," he said.

The onlookers refused to disband, following them to the rear of the shack. Slocum moved the muzzle of the Winchester around between Fairchild's shoulder blades and held it there.

"Put him forward up under the seat," John ordered. "Take off your coat and lay it over him. Cover his face."

Fairchild did so. Slocum hitched his and Ripley's horse to the tailgate and laying the rifle alongside the suitcase, mounted the seat beside the waiting Fairchild.

"Let's go, into town."

The swelling crowd watched in silence as the buckboard rattled away, the two horses trailing obediently.

"You did fine," said Slocum. "Keep playing it smart and you just may stay alive."

"Nearly fifty thousand dollars. A paltry fraction of what you can get if you're interested."

"I'm interested in getting you behind bars and, I hope, strung up alongside your brother."

Fairchild slapped the horse's rump with the reins and laughed thinly. "That, I'm afraid, you'll never see. It's very simple. I've done nothing to hang for. Tyson, perhaps, but not me. I didn't lynch Packer. I didn't even suggest it. It was all Tyson's idea."

"You are something, you know that? You'd hang everybody in sight if it meant saving your own neck!"

"You wouldn't? Life is sweet, John, well worth the holding onto. Particularly when you're as rich as I am."

"Yeah, you may be the richest man Texas ever strung up."

"As I was saying, the money in that suitcase is nickels and dimes. I can make you a full partner in the Welcomes, with more money than you ever dreamed of. And they're only the beginning. I'm negotiating for leases on six other wells. I'm not talking thousands—I mean millions. Ever fancy yourself a millionaire, John?"

"Ever fancy yourself dead from getting your mouth shot off for talking too much?"

They drove through the cacophony of hard-working pumps emerging from the fields and approaching the town.

"What are you doing with a suitcase fulla fifty thousand out there, for Christ's sake?"

"I had planned to leave for Houston to make a bank deposit just about when you showed up. I like night traveling. It's safer. I sell my oil for cash only, you see, no checks. I don't trust paper."

"You trust banks, though."

"I trust the First National in Houston. I'm on the board of directors."

"I must say you're a hard-working thief. Most crooks I know are lazy as snakes."

"Can we drive by the Yellow Rose? I'd like to pick up some clean clothes, my razor, toothbrush. You know."

"No time for that."

"It won't take but five minutes. I want to look civilized when I get to Goodnight."

"Just shut up and take no for the answer."

Moving slowly down the darkened street, Slocum ordered Fairchild to rein up in front of the funeral parlor. The place was dark.

"Get down and knock on the door," said Slocum.

"Mr. Abernathy's asleep. You don't see any lights."

"Knock on the door, dammit. Yell if you got to. Wake him up."

"If that's what you want."

Fairchild went to the door, raised his fist, paused, turned to Slocum, shrugged and knocked loudly. Reaching behind the seat, Slocum opened the snaps on the suitcase and flipped the lid. It was packed with money, fives and tens mostly, unbanded, sitting in stacks that filled the suitcase within an inch of one end.

"The son of a bitch!"

Closing it, he resnapped the latches.

"Mr. Abernathy?" called Fairchild.

A lamp showed upstairs, piercing the gloom. A short, thin man in his 60s, wearing a full-length nightshirt and cap, appeared at the door. Slocum got down and joined Fairchild.

"Mr. Abernathy, I got a body here I'd appreciate you'd take care of. A friend, a close friend," said Slocum.

"Mister, it's past one in the morning. I only been asleep an hour. I'm plumb exhausted."

"I'm sorry to wake you, but this gentleman here and myself are leaving town. We got to make the final arrangements for the deceased."

"I can't take on no more work. I laid out six corpses already tonight and I got fifteen more waitin' out back. There was trouble down to the Old Glory." He paused. "That's some-lookin' eye you got there. Is that the Old Glory?"

Slocum nodded.

"You ought to put a piece o' beefsteak on it."

"Yeah."

"I'm sorry about your friend."

"If you *could* lay him out, how much would you charge?"

"Depends. There's the three-dollar plain pine. There's all different grades lumber, different extras. The deluxe oak casket lay-out and burial combined I charge thirty-five dollars."

"I'll pay you two hundred."

"Two—" Abernathy gaped.

"Cash."

"Jesus Christ, I mean gosh! For two hundred you'd get the oak, a team o' mares with collar flowers, black and gilt four-side glass hearse, a six-piece mourning band, pallbearers, mourners, the works!"

"We don't need that." Slocum turned to Fairchild. "Bring him in. Make it fast."

Fairchild deposited Ripley's body on a sofa and stood by in silence as if awaiting further orders. Abernathy examined Ripley.

"He's been shot through the heart."

Slocum nodded. "Get the two hundred outta the suitcase," he said to Fairchild, jerking his thumb over his shoulder.

"Right."

"No, wait. That money belongs to Goodnight. Take out your billfold and pay the man."

"Really, John—"

"Really, Mr. Millionaire."

"The money in the suitcase, there's nearly fifty thousand. The depositors' money only totaled twenty-two—"

"Shut up, you son of a bitch, and pay the man!"

Fairchild shrugged and complied.

"You got a pencil and paper?" asked Slocum of Abernathy.

The undertaker opened a drawer and took out a pad with "ABERNATHY FUNERAL PARLOR—IF YOU WANT THE BEST WHEN LAID TO REST" printed across the top.

"Write this down," said Slocum. "I want you to lay him out in the best casket you got and freight it up to Houston with orders to send it on by rail to Humble City. That's Lea County, just over the border into New Mexico."

"Lea County. Got it. Care o' who?"

"Miss Florabelle Sachsenhauser, the Humble House, Humble City."

"How do you spell Sach—"

"Sachsenhauser. S—I guess, A—hell, don't ask me!"

Fairchild spelled the name. "I believe it's German, possibly Austrian."

Slocum waved him quiet. "I'll be sending a telegram to her explaining," he continued. "Just you see the body's shipped to her there. I'm trusting you two hundred bucks worth, mister."

"These directions'll be carried out to a 'T.' You got

my word o' honor on it. In all modesty I can say Jedediah Abernathy is as honest, as trustworthy and reliable as any banker you know."

"Shit!"

"Huh?"

"Nothing, forget it."

"I give you my word the body will be prepared, boxed, er, that is the deluxe oak flamingo-velvet interior casket will be provided, and the remains shipped in accordance with your wishes."

"I'm obliged to you."

Abernathy pocketed his pencil, tore the page from the pad, folded it once and slipped it inside Ripley's shirt pocket. Slocum and Fairchild left.

38

"Are we going to drive this buckboard all the way to Goodnight?" asked Fairchild disconsolately.

"No, you are."

"It's deucedly uncomfortable for such a long trek."

"Yeah."

Dawn was moments away, the sky brightening, a metallic gray overspreading it. The air became progressively sweeter to the taste as the miles multiplied between them and the fields. Seabirds wandering inland over the coastal plain soared and swooped overhead. The dust kicked up by the wagon wheels collected in a thick cloud behind them, obscuring view of the road over which they traveled.

They talked little, Fairchild initiating what conversation there was, and Slocum shutting him up abruptly every time.

The banker yawned. "I'm tired and starving," he complained. "Couldn't you go for a nice thick juicy steak?"

"We'll eat in a couple hours," said Slocum. "We gotta lot o' miles to make, and this mare and buckboard don't appear the fastest combination on wheels."

"I sincerely hope I can make it to a couple hours."

"Who are you kidding? You may look soft, but you carry plenty o' meat through the shoulders." He paused and narrowed his eyes at Fairchild. "And don't think I don't know what's running through your head. One way or another you fancy you're gonna get the drop on me."

"Would you believe me if I told you that's never entered my mind?"

"Hell no. Look up ahead there. That's a fairly steep rise for these parts. Pull over, we'll give your little girl a rest from the pulling." Fairchild geed the mare to the side of the road. "Get down, unshaft her and bring up the bay," said Slocum. "And don't take all day."

"You're the boss."

"That's me."

The switch was made, and they started up the rise. A sheer cliff rose to the left, its face catching the light of the rising sun, turning it the color of terra cotta. A hawk wheeled high, examining the earth below for mice and rabbits foraging breakfast.

The road widened at the summit, which overlooked a sheer 200-foot drop to a grass valley studded with pale-barked cottonwoods full of flickers and warblers, providing flashes of red and yellow.

A dozen yards from the top, Slocum's hand darted out, grabbing Fairchild's forearm. "Pull up."

"What?"

"Do it."

Fairchild pulled up hard, braking the buckboard to keep it from rolling back. A sound like gentle thunder was coming from the opposite side of the summit.

"Sounds like a goddamned army!" barked Slocum.

Riders appeared, four abreast, followed by more and more. Within seconds a crowd was assembled. Slocum glanced at Fairchild out of the corner of his eye. The banker had gone pale, biting his upper lip and toying nervously with the reins. One of the men at the front of the mob yelled in recognition and the entire crowd started down toward them.

"They're from Goodnight," said Fairchild tightly. "I recognize every one."

"The depositors?" Fairchild nodded grimly. "Oh, for Christ's sake!" A quick study and Slocum estimated there were close to 60 mounted men blocking the way, all recognizing Fairchild, all either glaring at him or smirking in triumph.

"Now ain't this enough to beat the mare down!" exclaimed a heavy-chested bearded man in the front line. "Boys, we ain't even got there and here we've found our man!"

Lifting his hand, he pulled it forward and the crowd followed him down. Coming up close, he grabbed the bay by the headstall.

"Hands off!" snapped Slocum, bringing up the rifle. Revealing it did not have quite the effect he wanted, however. Two things happened. The man let go of the headstall and everybody, him included, hauled iron, everything from handguns to rifles to shotguns, upward of 60 barrels pointing straight at Slocum.

"We'll take the man, fella," said the bearded man. "He belongs to us."

"Yeah," said the man alongside him. "We're gonna have us a party, and he's to be the guest of honor. Ain't that so, boys?"

The crowd roared agreement and a hand rose holding a neatly knotted noose.

"Hold everything," began Slocum.

"Hold shit, deputy!" exclaimed a tall blond man wearing his Stetson down his back and waving his .45 much too carelessly for Slocum's taste. "You give him over or we'll take him."

"And leave you face down in the road if we got to!" shouted another.

Again a roar of agreement. Worry—painful, annoying and decidely unwelcome—took firm hold of the pit of Slocum's stomach. If he handed him over, as sure as

God painted the sky the bastards would toss the noose around his neck. Six hands would grab the free end of the rope and over the side he'd go, kicked and pushed. Not that he didn't deserve it, but there was still the matter of a written confession. Without it, Judge Parfrey might have a sticky time trying to prove John Slocum wholly innocent and unwanted.

"You don't want him!" yelled Slocum.

"The hell we don't!"

"Before you fuck yourselves up for fair, you'd best make a choice. Decide which is more important, him dead or your money back. I mean every red cent, with interest!"

"We'll take both, mister," said the bearded one. The crowd cheered. "Let's cut out all this nonsense. Porter, give him the reins and get down."

"You want your money, you got it!" shouted Slocum. With this he picked up the suitcase, jumped to his feet and swinging it twice let it fly over the edge. It started down, hit an outcropping and burst open. Like oil gushing out of the top of a derrick, the mass of bills erupted, spreading in a great green cloud hanging suspended in the air for an instant, then fluttering slowly down into the valley.

Five dozen pairs of eyes stared, jaws dropped and the crowd turned to stone for the better part of three seconds. Somebody broke the spell with a shout. Then everybody yelled and action exploded. The whole troop wheeled about and thundered back down the way they'd come leaving a cloud of dust so thick Slocum could not see 20 feet ahead.

"Get down!" he snapped.

"What?"

"Do it! Get around back and untie Rip's horse! Stop gawking and move!"

As quickly as he had ever moved in his life, Slocum freed his bay from the shafts, saddled up, grabbed the rifle and took off through the slowly descending dust cloud, Fairchild clattering after him.

39

Marshal Elgin, the law in Loomis, was young but experienced, friendly, efficient and more than eager to cooperate with Judge Ira Parfrey. Disheveled and dirty, bone weary, Slocum sat in the marshal's surprisingly spacious office relating the events of the previous week, his charge already behind bars.

"Brother, you look beat down to the rowels," said Elgin sympathetically. "Why don't you lie down in one of the empties and catch yourself forty?"

"Thanks all the same, but tired as I am I don't imagine I'd sleep too well in a cell. Never have." He yawned. "Don't worry, I'll make it 'til night."

"Sorry about your pal."

"Yeah. Those things happen when lead starts buzzing around. Fella who shot him never knew he did." He hesitated, searching the marshal's eyes. "I don't mean to tell you your business or anything, marshal, but do you think it's best to stick Porter in the same cell with that brother o' his?"

Elgin grinned. "It's Ira's idea. He's already got a full written statement from Tyson, which all but blames Porter for everything from stealing the twenty-two thousand dollars to spitting on the sidewalk. Unless I'm dead wrong, the two of 'em are in there right now, babbling away like two biddies at a tea party. Ira figures and I agree that Porter's locked into the truth whether he likes it or not and them two talking will convince him."

"I sure wish the judge'd get back," said Slocum wistfully, staring out the barred window into the sun-drenched street. Elgin raised both feet to the cold wood stove, crossing ankles and resting them, tilting his chair back nonchalantly.

"He'll be by soon. He's over to Goodnight, seeing to them five what lynched your pal."

"Who's minding the store over there?"

"The deputies. New sheriff is supposed to be on his way down from Seven Wells. Hey, did you get your telegram off?"

"Soon. Before anything else, eating, sleeping even, I got to see Porter's confession on paper. I want to know where I stand."

"You stand fine, in the clear."

"I still want to see the paper."

"Brother, there's no way he can deny anything. Put it outta your mind, think about shaving."

A gig pulled up outside. Judge Parfrey. The door creaked open and his massive bulk blocked out the mid-afternoon sun.

"Welcome home, John Slocum."

"Howdy, your honor."

Judge Parfrey waved a handful of papers. "Statements from all five lynchers, signed and witnessed."

"Good," said Slocum. "Was it like I said? Did Tyson put 'em up to it?"

The judge nodded. "He paid them just as you figured. Billy Janes got fifty dollars and the others twenty-five." He shook his head and frowned. "Paying men to lynch, now that's a new wrinkle."

"Are you gonna take Porter's statement now?"

Elgin smiled, banging the floor with his heels and standing. "He's nervous as a cat that Porter's gonna clam up. Been fidgeting all over the place waiting for you."

"Take it easy, John. I'll get right at it."

"What about all the wanted dodgers?" asked Slocum.

"The word's out," Elgin said. "How it generally works is when a fresh dodger goes out, word of any people apprehended or cleared goes along with it. You needn't wait, you can go back to black hair. Just be thankful that picture o' you didn't read five thousand dollars dead or alive."

"Amen," said Judge Parfrey.

"What do you figure this mob'll get?" Slocum asked.

The judge rubbed his multiple chins and considered

the question. "Janes and his boys'll hang. Tyson ought to."

"What about Porter?"

"I don't know as he'll hang, but he'll go up for a long time. There's a loud public outcry against him all over the area, practically the entire town. There's a distinction there."

"What distinction?"

"A man robbing a bank is one thing, but a banker, a man people entrust with their savings, a man like that stealing, that's almost in the category of a crime against nature. It's going to go very hard for him." He placed the statements on Elgin's desk. "Let me go in and get his statement." Elgin took down the key ring from the peg over his desk, selected a key and handed it, with the ring dangling, to the judge. Parfrey started for the inner door, stopped and turned.

"What are your plans, John?"

Slocum shrugged. "I don't know. Guess I'll be moving on fairly soon."

"Do you have to?"

"Itchy feet, judge."

"The reason I ask is there's a lady who'd very much like to see you, cleanshaven, that is."

"Mrs. Weatherly."

The judge nodded. "You've made quite an impression on her."

"Mmmmm."

"Fine figure of a woman, Alice Weatherly. The sort that won't be a widow for long. She was a good wife to Seth. She'll make a good wife to any man."

"I reckon."

"Are you planning to shave?"

"What do you think?"

"Do. Get the trail dust out of your ears, come on back here and we'll show you a lovely looking piece of paper. Then maybe you'd like to ride over and see her."

"Maybe." Slocum got up, slapped dust out of his denims and sleeves, rubbed a careful hand over his beard and started out the door. "I'll be back. And thanks, judge, marshal. I purely appreciate all you've done."

They waved and he closed the door behind him. The street was lazy quiet, a lone couple in view crossing far up at the other end. A man slept in his tilted chair under a Mexican *sombrero* in front of the general store opposite. A mangy-looking terrier down off its legs was snoring by the hitching rail post. The breeze was elsewhere, the sky burning bright blue overhead. A typical hot, Texas-dry day better given to *siesta* than activity. Slocum yawned and stretched and cast an eye over his disreputable appearance.

Maybe the judge was right. Shave, clean up and after he'd gotten the telegram off to Florabelle Sachsenhauser and read over Porter's statement, he might just ride on out to the Weatherly spread.

She sure was some fine cook, Alice Weatherly.